READING COMPREHENSION OF COLLEGE ENGLISH BAND FOUR A NEW GUIDE TO TACKLE

大学英语全新四级阅读全方攻略

主 编 李 莉

副主编 张 艳 李立国 穆 琳
编 者 张 莹 张 磊 姚卫东

天津大学出版社
TIANJIN UNIVERSITY PRESS

图书在版编目(CIP)数据

大学英语全新四级阅读全方攻略/李莉主编.—天津:天津大学出版社,2008.5
ISBN 978-7-5618-2660-7

Ⅰ.大… Ⅱ.李… Ⅲ.英语 – 阅读教学 – 高等学校 – 水平考试 – 习题 Ⅳ.H319.4 – 44

中国版本图书馆 CIP 数据核字(2008)第 049484 号

出版发行	天津大学出版社
出 版 人	杨欢
地　　址	天津市卫津路 92 号天津大学内(邮编:300072)
电　　话	发行部:022-27403647　邮购部:022-27402742
网　　址	www.tjup.com
短信网址	发送"天大"至 916088
印　　刷	天津市泰宇印务有限公司
经　　销	全国各地新华书店
开　　本	169mm×239mm
印　　张	10
字　　数	246 千
版　　次	2008 年 5 月第 1 版
印　　次	2008 年 5 月第 1 次
印　　数	1 – 4 000
定　　价	20.00 元

前　言

　　全国大学英语四、六级考试委员会于 2006 年 10 月公布了《大学英语四级考试大纲》修订本。修订后的四级考试大纲对四级考试各部分测试内容、题型和所占分值比例进行了概述。四级试卷构成为：1)听力(占总分的 35％)；2)阅读理解，包括仔细阅读和快速阅读(占总分的 35％)；3)完型填空(占总分的 10％)；4)写作和翻译(占总分的 20％)。各单项报道分的满分分别为：听力 249 分，阅读 249 分，完型 70 分，写作和翻译 142 分。各单项分相加之和等于总分 710。

　　根据《大学英语四级考试大纲》修订本的要求，改革后的四级考试加大了阅读的难度，并增加了快速阅读，考生普遍反映对此不适应。鉴于此，本书依据改革后的四级题型，以及 2006 年和 2007 年的真题编写了八套全真模拟阅读试题。每套试题包括：1)快速阅读(Skimming and Scanning)；2)仔细阅读(Reading in Depth)。在给出答案的同时对试题进行了详细解析。

　　为使读者进一步熟悉改革后的四级题型，书后给出 2006 年 12 月、2007 年 6 月和 2007 年 12 月的大学英语四级真题共三套，并附有答案及听力原文。

　　本书难度循序渐进，既可作为课堂教学辅助教材使用，也适合学生自主学习。

　　参加编写的人员有：李莉、张艳、李立国、穆琳、张莹、张磊、姚卫东。

　　书中如有疏漏之处，望广大读者和同人提出宝贵意见。

编　者

2008 年 2 月

目　　录

Part I 模拟阅读试题

Model Test 1

Part I **Reading Comprehension** (**Skimming and Scanning**) (**15 minutes**)

Directions: *In this part, you will have 15 minutes to go over the passage quickly and answer the questions on **Answer Sheet** 1.*

For questions 1 ~ 7, mark

Y (*for YES*)   *if the statement agrees with the information given in the passage;*

N (*for NO*)   *if the statement contradicts the information given in the passage;*

NG (*for NOT GIVEN*)   *if the information is not given in the passage.*

For questions 8 ~ 10, complete the sentences with the information given in the passage.

Will We Run Out of Water?

Picture a "ghost ship" sinking into the sand, left to rot on dry land by a receding sea. Then imagine dust storms sweeping up toxic pesticides and chemical fertilizers from the dry seabed and spewing them across towns and villages.

Seem like a scene from a movie about the end of the world? For people living near the *Aral Sea* (咸海) in Central Asia, it's all too real. Thirty years ago, government planners diverted the rivers that flow into the sea in order to irrigate (provide water for) farmland. As a result, the sea has shrunk to half its original size, *stranding* (使搁浅) ships on dry land. The seawater has tripled in salt content and become polluted, killing all 24 native species of fish.

Similar large-scale efforts to redirect water in other parts of the world have also ended in ecological crisis, according to numerous environmental groups. But many countries continue to build massive dams and irrigation systems, even though such projects can create more problems than they fix. Why? People in many parts of the world are desperate for water, and more people will need more water in the next century.

"Growing populations will worsen problems with water," says Peter H. Gleick, an environmental scientist at the Pacific Institute for studies in Development, Environment, and Security, a research organization in California. He fears that by the year 2025, as many as one third of the world's *projected* (预测的) 8.3 billion people will suffer from water shortages.

WHERE WATER GOES

Only 2.5 percent of all water on Earth is freshwater, water suitable for drinking and growing food, says Sandra Postel, director of the Global Water Policy Project in Amherst, Mass. Two thirds of this freshwater is locked in *glaciers* (冰山) and *ice caps* (冰盖). In fact, only a tiny percentage of freshwater is part of the water cycle, in which water evaporates and rises into the atmosphere, then condenses and falls back to Earth as precipitation (rain or snow).

Some precipitation runs off land to lakes and oceans, and some becomes groundwater, water that seeps into the earth. Much of this renewable freshwater ends up in remote places like the Amazon river basin in Brazil, where few people live. In fact, the world's population has access to only 12,500 cubic kilometers of freshwater—about the amount of water in *Lake Superior* (苏必利尔湖). And people use half of this amount already. "If water demand continues to climb rapidly," says Postel, "there will be severe shortages and damage to the *aquatic* (水的) environment."

CLOSE TO HOME

Water *woes* (灾难) may seem remote to people living in rich countries like the United States. But Americans could face serious water shortages, too especially in areas that rely on groundwater. Groundwater accumulates in *aquifers* (地下蓄水层), layers of sand and gravel that lie between soil and bedrock. (For every liter of surface water, more than 90 liters are hidden underground.) Although the United States has large aquifers, farmers, ranchers, and cities are tapping many of them for water faster than nature can *replenish* (补充) it. In northwest Texas, for example, over-pumping has shrunk groundwater supplies by 25 percent, according to Postel.

Americans may face even more urgent problems from pollution. Drinking water in the United States is generally safe and meets high standards. Nevertheless, one in five Americans every day unknowingly drinks tap water contaminated with bacteria and chemical wastes, according to the Environmental Protection Agency. In Milwaukee, 400,000 people fell ill in 1993 after drinking tap water tainted with *cryptosporidium* (隐孢子虫), a *microbe* (微生物) that causes fever, *diarrhea* (腹泻) and vomiting.

THE SOURCE

Where so contaminants come from? In developing countries, people dump *raw* (未经处理的) *sewage* (污水) into the same streams and rivers from which they draw water for drinking and cooking; about 250 million people a year get sick from water *borne* (饮水传染的) diseases.

In developed countries, manufacturers use 100,000 chemical compounds to make a wide range of products. Toxic chemicals pollute water when released untreated into rivers and lakes. (Certain compounds, such as polychlorinated *biphenyls* (多氯化联二苯), or PCBs, have been banned in the United States.)

But almost everyone contributes to water pollution. People often pour household cleaners, car antifreeze, and paint *thinners* (稀释剂) down the drain; all of these contain hazardous chemicals. Scientists studying water in the San Francisco Bay reported in 1996 that 70 percent of the pollutants could be traced to household waste.

Farmers have been criticized for overusing herbicides and pesticides, chemicals that kill weeds and insects but that pollute water as well. Farmers also use nitrates, nitrogen—rich fertilizer that helps plants grow but that can wreak *havoc* (大破坏) on the environment. Nitrates are swept away by surface runoff to lakes and seas. Too many nitrates "over-enrich" these bodies of water, encouraging the buildup of algae, or microscopic plants that live on the surface of the water. Algae deprive the water of oxygen that fish need to survive, at times choking off life in an entire body of water.

WHAT'S THE SOLUTION?

Water expert Gleick advocates conservation and local solutions to water-related problems; governments, for instance, would be better off building small-scale dams rather than huge and disruptive projects like the one that ruined the Aral Sea.

"More than 1 billion people worldwide don't have access to basic clean drinking water," says Gleick. "There has to be a strong push on the part of everyone—governments and ordinary people—to make sure we have a resource so fundamental to life."

1. That the huge water projects have diverted the rivers causes the Aral Sea to shrink.
2. The construction of massive dams and irrigation projects does more good than harm.
3. The chief causes of water shortage are population growth and water pollution.
4. The problems Americans face concerning water are ground water shrinkage and tap water pollution.
5. According to the passage all water pollutants come from household waste.
6. The people living in the United States will not be faced with water shortages.
7. Water expert Gleick has come up with the best solution to water-related problems.
8. According to Peter H. Gleick, by the year 2025, as many as _____ of the world's people will suffer from water shortages.
9. Two thirds of the freshwater on Earth is locked in _____ .
10. In developed countries, before toxic chemicals are released into rivers and lakes, they should be treated in order to avoid _____ .

Part II Reading Comprehension (Reading in Depth) (25 minutes)
Section A
Directions: *In this section, there is a passage with ten blanks. You are required to select one*

4

*word for each blank from a list of choices given in a word bank following the passage. Read the passage through carefully before making your choices. Each choice in bank is identified by a letter. Please mark the corresponding letter for each item on **Answer Sheet 2** with a single line through the center. **You may not use any of the words in the bank more than once.***

Questions 11 to 20 are based on the following passage.

If our society ever needed a reading *renaissance*（复兴）, it's now. The National Endowment for the Arts released "Reading at Risk" last year, a study showing that adult reading ___11___ have dropped 10 percentage points in the past decade, with the steepest drop among those 18 to 24. "Only one half of young people read a book of any kind in 2002. We set the bar almost on the ground. If you read one short story in a teenager magazine, that would have ___12___," laments a director of research and analysis. He ___13___ the loss of readers to the booming world of technology, which attracts would-be leisure readers to E-mail, IM chats, and video games and leaves them with no time to cope with a novel.

"These new forms of media undoubtedly have some benefits," says Steven Johnson, author of *Everything Bad Is Good for You*. Video games ___14___ problem-solving skills; TV shows promote mental gymnastics by ___15___ viewers to follow complex story lines. But books offer experience that can't be gained from these other sources, from ___16___ vocabulary to stretching the imagination. "If they're not reading at all," says Johnson, "that's a huge problem." In fact, fewer kids are reading for pleasure. According to data ___17___ last week from the National Center for Educational Statistic's long-term trend assessment, the number of 17-year-olds who reported never or hardly ever reading for fun ___18___ from 9 percent in 1984 to 19 percent in 2004. At the same time, the ___19___ of 17-year-olds who read daily dropped from 31 to 22.

This slow but steady retreat from books has not yet taken a toll on reading ability. Scores for the nation's youth have ___20___ constant over the past two decades (with an encouraging upswing among 9-year-olds). But given the strong apparent correlation between pleasure reading and reading skills, this means poorly for the future.

A. percent	I. believing
B. remained	J. released
C. rose	K. forcing
D. rates	L. improve
E. percentage	M. styles
F. counted	N. building
G. relieved	O. attributes
H. present	

Section B

Directions: *There are 2 passages in this section. Each passage is followed by some questions or* *unfinished statements. For each of them there are four choices marked A, B, C, D and You should decide on the best choice and mark the corresponding letter on **Answer Sheet** 2 with a single line through the center.*

Passage One

Questions 21 to 25 are based on the following passage.

There is a new type of small advertisement becoming increasingly common in newspaper classified columns. It is sometimes placed among "situations vacant", although it does not offer anyone a job, and sometimes it appears among "situations wanted", although it is not placed by someone looking for a job, either. What it does is to offer help in applying for a job.

"Contact us before writing your application", or "Make use of our long experience in preparing your curriculum vitae or job history", is how it is usually expressed. The growth and apparent success of such a specialized service is, of course, a reflection on the current high levels of unemployment. It is also an indication of the growing importance of the curriculum vitae (or job history), with the suggestion that it may now qualify as an art form in its own right.

There was a time when job seekers simply wrote letters of application. "Just put down your name, address, age and whether you have passed any exams", was about the average level of advice offered to young people applying for their first jobs when I left school. The letter was really just for openers, it was explained, everything else could and should be saved for the interview. And in those days of full employment the technique worked. The letter proved that you could write and were available for work. Your eager face and intelligent replies did the rest.

Later, as you moved up the ladder, something slightly more sophisticated was called for. The advice then was to put something in the letter which would distinguish you from the rest. It might be the aggressive approach. "Your search is over. I am the person you are looking for", was a widely used trick that occasionally succeeded. Or it might be some special feature specially designed for the job interview.

There is no doubt, however, that it is increasing number of applicants with university education at all points in the process of engaging staff that has led to the greater importance of the curriculum vitae.

21. The new type of advertisement which is appearing in newspaper columns _____.

A. informs job hunters of the opportunities available

B. promises to offer useful advice to those looking for employment

C. divides available jobs into various types

D. informs employers of the people available for work

22. Nowadays a demand for this specialized type of service has been created because _____.

A. there is a lack of jobs available for artistic people

6

B. there are so many top level jobs available

C. there are so many people out of work

D. the job history is considered to be a work of art

23. In the past it was expected that first job hunters would _____.

A. write an initial letter giving their life history

B. pass some exams before applying for a job

C. have no qualifications other than being able to read and write

D. keep any detailed information until they obtained an interview

24. Later, as one went on to apply for more important jobs, one was advised to include in the letter _____.

A. something that would distinguish one from other applicants

B. hinted information about the personality of the applicant

C. one's advantages over others in applying for the job

D. an occasional trick with the aggressive approach

25. The curriculum vitae has become such an important document because _____.

A. there has been an increase in the number of jobs advertised

B. there has been an increase in the number of applicants with degrees

C. jobs are becoming much more complicated nowadays

D. the other processes of applying for jobs are more complicated

Passage Two

Questions 26 to 30 are based on the following passage.

In cities with rent control, the city government sets the maximum rent that a landlord can charge for an apartment. Supporters of rent control argue that it protects people who are living in apartments. Their rent cannot increase; therefore, they are not in danger of losing their homes. However, the critics say that after a long time, rent control may have negative effects. Landlords know that they cannot increase their profits. Therefore, they invest in other businesses where they can increase their profits. They do not invest in new buildings which would also be rent-controlled. As a result, new apartments are not built. Many people who need apartments cannot find any. According to the critics, the end result of rent control is a shortage of apartments in the city.

Some theorists argue that the minimum wage law can cause problems in the same way. The federal government sets the minimum that an employer must pay workers. The minimum helps people who generally look for unskilled, low-paying jobs. However, if the minimum is high, employers may hire fewer workers. They will replace workers with machinery. The price, which is the wage that employers must pay, increases. Therefore, other things being equal, the number of workers that employers want decreases. Thus, critics claim, an increase in the minimum wage may cause unemployment. Some poor people may find themselves without jobs instead of with jobs at the minimum wage.

Supporters of the minimum wage say that it helps people keep their dignity. Because of the law, workers cannot sell their services for less than the minimum. Furthermore, employers cannot force workers to accept jobs at unfair wages.

Economic theory predicts the results of economic decisions such as decisions about farm production, rent control, and the minimum wage. The predictions may be correct only if "other things are equal". Economists do not agree on some of the predictions. They also do not agree on the value of different decisions. Some economists support a particular decision while others criticize it. Economists do agree, however, that there are no simple answers to economic questions.

26. There is the possibility that setting maximum rent may _____.

A. cause a shortage of apartments

B. worry those who rent apartments as homes

C. increase the profits of landlords

D. encourage landlords to invest in building apartment

27. According to the critics, rent control _____.

A. will always benefit those who rent apartments

B. is unnecessary

C. will bring negative effects in the long run

D. is necessary under all circumstances

28. The problem of unemployment will arise _____.

A. if the minimum wage is set too high   B. if the minimum wage is set too low

C. if the workers are unskilled   D. if the maximum wage is set

29. The passage tells us _____.

A. the relationship between supply and demand

B. the possible results of government controls

C. the necessity of government control

D. the urgency of getting rid of government controls

30. Which of the following statements is NOT true?

A. The results of economic decisions can not always be predicted.

B. Minimum wage can not always protect employees.

C. Economic theory can predict the results of economic decisions if other factors are not changing.

D. Economic decisions should not be based on economic theory.

Model Test 2

Part I Reading Comprehension (Skimming and Scanning) (**15 minutes**)

Directions: *In this part, you will have **15** minutes to go over the passage quickly and answer the questions on **Answer Sheet 1**.*

For questions 1 ~ 7, mark

Y (*for YES*)   *if the statement agrees with the information given in the passage;*

N (*for NO*)   *if the statement contradicts the information given in the passage;*

NG (*for NOT GIVEN*)   *if the information is not given in the passage.*

For questions 8 ~ 10, complete the sentences with the information given in the passage.

When we think of entrepreneurs, most of us imagine dynamic, successful, over-achievers like Bill Gates of Microsoft, Richard Branson of Virgin Airlines, Inc. or Jim Boyle of Columbia Sportswear, to name a few contemporary heroes. The truth is that we often fail to recognize entrepreneurs all around us: the corner grocery store owner, the family physician who opens a medical practice in our neighborhood, or the young person who delivers the morning paper. Each is creating business opportunities through entrepreneurship, although the process of entrepreneurship would be markedly different from each other.

According to Jeffery Timmons, author of "New Venture Creation" (1990), there are three crucial components for a successful new venture: the opportunity, the entrepreneur, and the resources needed to start the company and make it grow. The opportunity is the idea for a new business. The entrepreneur is the person who develops the idea for a business into a business. Resources include money, people and skill. In this unit, we focus on entrepreneurs, one of the critical ingredients for success of a new business: Who are they? What makes them tick?

One factor which distinguishes Bill Gates from the morning paper deliverer is the level of business success each desires to achieve. Determining what success means to you is a crucial element in the early stages of new venture planning. How you measure success in life shapes your views of business opportunities and small business. We begin this unit with a look at success: what it means and how it is measured.

Defining Success through Personal Evaluation

"Most people spend less time planning their new business than they do their family vacation" (*Canadian Small Business*, 1997). Yet, selecting the right business idea and planning for its success are crucial steps in new venture planning. You will learn more about opportunity identification, or how to find and evaluate business ideas. For now, let's focus on success.

Success is how you define it. What success means to you will not likely be what success means to someone else. Success is very personal and subjective. We usually measure success in one or three ways:

Success can be measured in dollars, usually earnings.

Success can be measured by the value of our possessions, including our home.

Success can be measured through our personal values.

Whether you define success by money, possessions, personal values or a combination of the three is up to you? How we define success significantly influences our selection of a business to start. Our view of success becomes our framework for evaluating business opportunities. If we think a business opportunity has the potential to raise us to our desired level of success, we give it further consideration. If not, we usually discard the idea. For example, if the paper deliverer defined success as earning $75.00 of spending money per month and he or she was earning $200.00 per month, then they would consider their venture highly successful.

Visioning and Goal-Setting for Business Success

Planning for business success begins with an understanding of ourselves, who we are and where we want to go in our professional lives. Enrolling in college is one step toward fulfilling our vision of the future. Two processes which are helpful to would-be entrepreneurs are visioning and goal-setting.

Success begins with a vision of who we are, what drives us and what we want. The vision of ourselves is the foundation that will give us guidance and direction in the conduct of our lives and business. Visioning involves development of a clear mental picture of what we would like to become in the next five to ten years.

Goal-setting involves developing a list of things you would like to achieve in your personal or professional lives—your goals. Goal-setting is the action plan for achieving your vision of life. According to the authors of *Canadian Small Business*, goals should be "SMART", i.e. Specific, Measurable, Achievable, Realistic, and Time-oriented.

Entrepreneurship begins with an understanding of who we are and where we want to go. For millions of Canadians, starting a business of their own was the path chosen to get them where they wanted to go. Understanding what success means to you and the level of success you are willing to accept in life is one of the first stages of new venture planning. Visioning and goal-setting are tools you can use to develop a clear picture of who you are, where you are going and what you need to do to get there.

1. Both the family physician who opens a medical practice in our neighborhood and the young

person who delivers the morning paper are not entrepreneurs.

2. The essential elements for a successful new venture are opportunity, entrepreneur and resources.

3. The resources needed to start the company and make it grow include money, practice and skill.

4. The difference between Bill Gates and the paper deliverer is the level of business success each desires to achieve.

5. The definition of success helps to evaluate the business potential effectively.

6. Going abroad for a further study also helps to fulfill one's vision of the future.

7. Goal-setting is the action plan for achieving your vision of life.

8. If we don't think a business opportunity has the potential to raise us to our desired level of success, we usually _____ .

9. The vision of ourselves is the foundation that will give us _____ in the conduct of our lives and business.

10. Visioning and goal-setting are _____ used to identify oneself and achieve one's purpose.

Part II Reading Comprehension (Reading in Depth) (25 minutes)
Section A

Directions: *In this section, there is a passage with ten blanks. You are required to select one word for each blank from a list of choices given in a word bank following the passage. Read the passage through carefully before making your choices. Each choice in bank is identified by a letter. Please mark the corresponding letter for each item on **Answer Sheet 2** with a single line through the center. **You may not use any of the words in the bank more than once**.*

Questions 11 to 20 are based on the following passage.

Global warming is real. The five warmest years since good records began to be kept have all been in this decade.

If you ever live ___11___ an average Chicago winter, a little bit of global warming doesn't sound bad. But one of the implications of global worming is an ___12___ in storms. Studies have reported a 20% increase in ___13___ storms in recent years.

Another ___14___ of global warming is a steady ___15___ of glaciers around the world, and that's well documented. Big chunks of the Atlantic ice cap are breaking off and ___16___ away; every major glacier in the Northern Hemisphere is retreating; the icy ___17___ of the Andes in South America are disappearing, an unpleasant circumstance for the farmers who ___18___ on melting water to grow their crops.

It has been suggested that all this melting ice will ___19___ sea levels. So it will, but

11

there's a more immediate problem. There's an awful lot of real estate now used by human beings that lies only a foot or less __20__ sea level; a good bit of that will be flooded:

A. severe	I. release
B. floating	J. through
C. function	K. apply
D. raise	L. rely
E. increase	M. consequence
F. consider	N. solution
G. melting	O. above
H. summits	

Section B

Directions: *There are 2 passages in this section. Each passage is followed by some questions or unfinished statement. For each of them there are four choices marked A, B, C and D. You should decide on the best choice and mark the corresponding letter on **Answer Sheet 2** with a single line through the center.*

Passage One

Questions 21 to 25 are based on the following passage.

Learning disabilities are very common. They affect perhaps 10 percent of all children. Four times as many boys as girls have learning disabilities.

Since about 1970, new research has helped brain scientists understand these problems better. Scientists now know there are many different kinds of learning disabilities and that they are caused by many different things. There is no longer any question that all learning disabilities result from differences in the way the brain is organized.

You cannot look at a child and tall if he or she has a learning disability. There is no outward sign of the disorder. So some researchers began looking at the brain itself to learn what might be wrong.

In one study, researchers examined the brain of a learning-disabled person who had died in an accident. They found two unusual things. One involved cells in the left side of the brain, which control language. These cells normally were white. In the learning-disabled person, however, these cells were gray. The researchers also found that many of the nerve cells were not in a line the way they should have been. The nerve cells were mixed together.

The study was carried out under the guidance of Norman Geschwind, and early expert on learning disabilities. Doctor Geschwind proposed that learning disabilities resulted mainly from problems in the left side of the brain. He believed this side of the brain failed to develop normally. Probably, he said, nerve cells there did not connect as they should. So the brain was like an electrical device in which the wires were crossed.

12

Other researches did not examine brain tissue. Instead, they measured the brain's electrical activity and made a man of the electrical signals.

Frank Duffy experimented with this technique at Children's Hospital Medical Center in Boston. Doctor Duffy said his research is evidence that reading disabilities involve damage to wide area of the brain, not just the left side.

21. Scientists found that the brain cells of a learning-disabled person differ from those of a normal person in _____ .

A. structure and function   B. color and function

C. size and arrangement   D. color and arrangement

22. Which of the following is NOT mentioned in the passage?

A. Learning disabilities may result from the unknown area of the brain.

B. Learning disabilities may result from damage to a wide area of the brain.

C. Learning disabilities may result from abnormal organization of brain cells.

D. Learning disabilities may result from problems in the left side of the brain.

23. All of the following statements are true except that _____ .

A. many factors account for learning disorder

B. a learning-disabled person shows no outward signs

C. reading disabilities are a common problem that affects 10 percent of the population

D. the brain activity of learning-disabled children is different from that of normal children

24. Doctor Duffy believed that _____ .

A. he found the exact cause of learning disabilities

B. the problem of learning disabilities was not limited to the left side of the brain

C. the problem of learning disabilities resulted from the left side of the brain

D. the problem of learning disabilities did not lie in the left side of the brain

25. According to the passage we can conclude that further researches should be made

_____ .

A. to investigate possible influences on brain development and organization

B. to study how children learn to read and write, and use numbers

C. to help learning-disabled children to develop their intelligence

D. to explore how the left side of the brain functions in language learning

Passage Two

Questions 26 to 30 are based on the following passage.

In 1985, the Coca-Cola company made the decision to change the formula of its leading soft drink. The change was based on the findings of many market studies. These studies had shown that the general response to the new product was good. However, the change of the traditional Coca-Cola by New Coke was rejected by the majority of drinkers. In fact, the company had to step back and restart production of the old formula of Coca-Cola.

The most important reason why New Coke was rejected was the emotional relationship that existed between drinkers and the old soft drink formula. Drinking Coca-Cola had become a tradition for many people over its 99 years of existence. The change made by the company was not only in Coke's formula but also in the traditional values and memories that it represented to the drinkers. "We had taken away more than the product Coca-Cola. We had taken away a little part of them and their past." The drinkers rejected this "improvement" because "they believed that Coke stood for traditional value, so they felt betrayed when the product changed completely overnight".

Although a lot of research was done by Coca-Cola company, it didn't show the depth of drinkers' emotion for the product. The studies took many forms, but none of the tests was able to measure the degree of personal and emotional reactions caused by the disappearance of the old, traditional Coca-Cola. The weakness of the research was that it was mainly quantitative in form. The result was only numbers that could not show the deep meaning the product had for many people. A more extensive study focusing on the qualitative aspects of the change would perhaps have been able to demonstrate the close relationship existing between drinkers and product.

26. Coca-Cola company changed the formula in 1985 because _____ .

A. it was rejected by the majority of drinkers

B. its market studies supported the change in the formula

C. it carried out many market research for expansion

D. it simply felt the need to make the change

27. According to the passage, the drinkers rejected New Coke because of _____ .

A. late response to the market by Coca-Cola company

B. reproduction of Coca-Cola's old drink formula

C. strong dislike by Coca-Cola's regular drinkers

D. emotional relationship between drinkers and the old soft drink

28. Coca-Cola product was believed to stand for _____ .

A. traditional values and good memories   B. traditional customs and happy days

C. past honors and efficient management   D. top quality and wonderful taste

29. Which of the following statements is true?

A. Research by Coca-Cola considered emotional factors.

B. Coca-Cola did not carry out sufficient research.

C. Research by Coca-Cola was quantitative rather than qualitative.

D. Research by Coca-Cola was both quantitative and qualitative.

30. The author of the article clearly indicates that _____ .

A. the weakness of the research could have been removed

B. Coca-Cola should have measured the quantitative factors more carefully

C. Coca-Cola should have done a more extensive qualitative study

D. a slower change of the product might have improved the sales of the company

Model Test 3

Part I   Reading Comprehension (Skimming and Scanning) (**15 minutes**)
Directions: *In this part*, *you will have 15 minutes to go over the passage quickly and answer the questions on* ***Answer Sheet 1***.
For questions 1 ~ 7, *mark*
Y (***for YES***)   *if the statement agrees with the information given in the passage*;
N (***for NO***)   *if the statement contradicts the information given in the passage*;
NG (***for NOT GIVEN***)   *if the information is not given in the passage*.
For questions 8 ~ 10, *complete the sentences with the information given in the passage*.

Marriage guidance counselors never stop hearing it. "He (or She) never listens", warring couples complain, again and again, as if they were chanting a *mantra*(吟颂祷文). And it is the same at work. Bosses say it of executives they are displeased with, and the executives return the compliment with interest when complaining about their bosses. Customers say it about suppliers who have cocked up, and suppliers—having patiently explained why on this occasion they cannot provide exactly what is wanted—say the same about their customers. Like married couples, we all shout the accusation at others, pretending that we ourselves are faultless.

Yet in our hearts we know many of the mistakes we make come about because we haven't listened sufficiently carefully. We get things wrong because we haven't quite understood what was wanted, or haven't figure out the implications of what we were told. Anyone who has ever written the minutes of a long meeting will know how hard it is to remember—even with the benefit of notes—exactly what everyone said and, more importantly, exactly what everyone meant. But success depends on getting things right and that means listening: listening, listening, listening.

Hearing is not listening. Listening is not a passive activity. It is a hard work. It demands attention and concentration. It may mean probing the speaker for additional information. If you allow your mind to wander, even for a few minutes, you'll naturally miss what the speaker is saying—probably at the very moment when the speaker is saying something crucial. But not having heard, you won't know what you've missed until too late.

The most common bad habit we all have is to start thinking of what we are going to say long before the other speaker has finished. Then we stop listening.

Worse still, this often adds rudeness to inattentiveness, as once you have determined what

16

you intend to say there is a fair chance you will rudely butt in on the other person to say it. The American wit Letitia Baldridge said, "Good listeners don't interrupt ever—unless the building's on fire". It's a good rule of thumb.

One of the key ways to improve your listening ability is by learning to keep a watchful eye on the speakers' body language. The ways people move and position themselves while they are speaking can reveal a great deal about what they are saying. Being a good listener involves being a good watcher: eyes and ears must go hand in hand.

For example, people who cover up their mouths with their hands while they are speaking are usually betraying insecurity, and may well be lying. When people rub their noses, it generally indicates they are puzzled; when they shrug their shoulders they are indifferent; when they hug themselves they are feeling threatened. If they are smiling as they speak they want you to feel the message is friendly, even if its content sounds hostile. On the other hand, if they are clenching their fists and drumming their fingers they may be restraining their anger, and may be much more furious than their words suggest.

The American psychologist Robert C. Beck, who has specialized in research into how people can teach themselves to be a better listeners, offers the following half-dozen rules for self-improvement.

Be patient—accept that many people are not very good communicators, encourage them to make things crystal clear, and don't interrupt impatiently or jump to conclusions.

Be empathetic—put yourself in the other's person's shoes, both intellectually and emotionally; it will help you understand what they are getting at.

Don't be too clever—faced with a know-all, many people become silent, either because they don't want to look foolish or because they see no point in bothering to continue.

Use self-disclosure—admitting to your own problems and difficulties, and to your own mistakes, will encourage people to speak openly and honestly about theirs.

Ask for explanations—get people to explain points or words you have not fully understood; it is always better to ask them to press on regardless—and then get things wrong.

Ask "opening up" questions—these are gentle, unthreatening and open-ended; they cannot be answered with a mere "yes" or "no" and should provide no clues as to the answer the questioner might want to hear.

Finally, it is almost always worth summing up the central idea of what you have just been told, as quickly and briefly as you can, before the discussion ends. Nobody is ever offended by having what they have just said repeated to them. It ensures you have listened accurately and grasped the correct messages. Of things go pear-shaped thereafter, at least the pears can't be dumped on your doorstep.

1. When people say "He (or She) never listens", they mean that he (or she) should take the blame.

2. Listening is different from hearing in that it demands more additional information.

3. To be a good listener, your eyes and ears must go hand in hand.

4. If someone looks straight at the speaker, with the eyes becoming slightly unfocused, it generally indicates that he feels bored.

5. Don't interrupt impatiently or jump to conclusions when communicating with other people.

6. Most people would become much more communicative while they are talking to a clever person.

7. Get people to explain points of words you have not fully understood during the conversation.

8. We all shout the accusation at others, pretending that we ourselves are _____ .

9. One of the essential ways to develop your listening ability is to watch _____ carefully.

10. Summarizing the central idea of what you have just been told quickly and briefly ensures you have listened accurately and _____ .

Part II　Reading Comprehension (Reading in Depth) (25 minutes)
Section A

Directions: *In this section, there is a passage with ten blanks. You are required to select one word for each blank from a list of choices given in a word bank following the passage. Read the passage through carefully before making your choices. Each choice in bank is identified by a letter. Please mark the corresponding letter for each item on* **Answer Sheet 2** *with a single line through the center.* ***You may not use any of the words in the bank more than once.***

Questions 11 to 20 are based on the following passage.

Everyone wants to be healthy and happy. __11__ , illness or accidents may occur without any warning. Frequently the person who is ill can be cared for at home if there is someone __12__ of looking after him under the doctor's direction. Sometimes arrangements can be made for a visiting nurse to give the necessary __13__ once a day or oftener, if necessary. The responsible one in the home carries on with the rest of the care during the __14__ between the nurses' visits.

The rapid diagnosis and immediate treatment on the spot of an accident or sudden illness, while awaiting the arrival of doctors, is called the first aid and quite __15__ from the home nursing.

When illness does come, the whole family is __16__ . Many adjustments have to be made but the family routine needn't be __17__ completely. Often it can be rearranged with home duties simplified to save time and energy thus reducing __18__ on the family.

The reasonable responsibility for giving nursing care is usually   19   by one person, frequently the mother.   20   , in order that she may have some much needed rest or on the contrary other members of the family should learn how to help when sickness occurs.

A. interval	I. efficient
B. capable	J. strain
C. occasion	K. unfortunately
D. disturbed	L. assumed
E. moreover	M. however
F. obtain	N. distinct
G. treatment	O. affected
H. worry	

Section B

Directions: *There are 2 passages in this section. Each passage is followed by some questions or unfinished statement. For each of them there are four choices marked A, B, C and D. You should decide on the best choice and mark the corresponding letter on* **Answer Sheet 2** *with a single line through the center.*

Passage One

Questions 21 to 25 are based on the following passage.

Managers of most businesses want high profits in order to pay high dividends to investors. For this reason, they aim to keep costs as low as possible. They also want to set high prices to gain high revenues. But competition within the industry often prevents them from doing so. Generally, a business will not increase the price of its output if its competitors will not increase their prices. If a business sets its prices higher than those of its rivals, many of its customers will buy the output of its rivals.

An important decision managers make is their choice of input-mix — what combination of capital, labor, and raw materials to use in production. The object is to keep production costs as low as possible. If labor costs are high, for example, a firm may invest in automatic machinery so that fewer workers are needed to accomplish the same task. If labor is cheap, the company may decide to employ extra workers instead of buying a machine to do the job. The combination of inputs that permits a firm to produce its goods or services at the lowest possible cost without reducing quality is called the most productive input-mix.

The goal of keeping production costs low also affects a company's choice of location. The resources an industry needs and the customers it serves are rarely close to each other. As a result, a business must transport inputs, outputs, or both. A business also tries to keep transportation costs as low as possible.

Transportation costs are based on weight and bulk as well as on distance. The location a company selects may thus depend on whether the company's product is heavier or lighter than the materials used to make it. The soft drink industry, which adds water to other ingredients to make its products, is an example of an industry that produces weight-gaining products. Soft drink companies choose locations near their customers. The paper industry is an example of industries that produce weight-losing products. Many such industries are near sources of raw materials.

21. What do business choose to do about the prices of their products in competition?

A. Set higher prices.   B. Leave the prices unchanged.

C. Offer lower prices.   D. Keep the prices adjustable.

22. The phrase "the most productive input-mix" means mixing inputs _____.

A. to produce goods or services at the lowest possible cost

B. through selling goods or services at the lowest possible prices

C. with goods or services sold at the lowest possible prices

D. to produce quality goods or services at the lowest possible cost

23. Why is a company usually very carefully about choosing its location?

A. Because the materials it needs are rather far away.

B. Because the customers it serves are not so close.

C. Because its resources and customers are seldom close to each other.

D. Because both production and transportation costs are rather high.

24. The soft drink industry and the paper making industry are used as examples because _____ _____.

A. they are different from each other B. they share a lot in common

C. they are both making lower profits D. they transport their products at the same costs

25. What is the writer of this passage attempting to do?

A. Explain what input-mix means.

B. Indicate how a business lowers its production costs to be more competitive.

C. Show how a business should set its prices in competition.

D. Explain how a business chooses its location.

Passage Two

Questions 26 to 30 are based on the following passage.

Beauty has always been regarded as something praise worthy. Almost everyone thinks attractive people are happier and healthier, have better marriages and respectable occupations. Personal consultants give them better advice for finding jobs. Even judges are softer on attractive *defendants*(被告). But in the executive circle, beauty can become a liability.

While attractiveness is a positive factor for a man on his way up the executive ladder, it is harmful to a woman.

Handsome male executives were perceived as having more integrity than plainer men; effort and ability were thought to account for their success.

Attractive female executives were considered to have less integrity than unattractive ones; their success was attributed not to ability but to factors such as luck.

All unattractive women executives were thought to have more integrity and to be more capable than the attractive female executives. Interestingly, though, the rise of the unattractive overnight successes was attributed more to personal relationships and less to ability than was that of attractive overnight successes.

Why are attractive women not thought to be able? An attractive woman is perceived to be more *feminine*(女性的)and an attractive man more *masculine*(男性的)than the less attractive ones. Thus, an attractive woman has an advantage in traditionally female jobs, but an attractive woman in a traditionally masculine position appears to lack the "masculine" qualities required.

This is true even in politics. "When the only clue is how he or she looks, people treat men and women differently", says Anne Bowman, who recently published a study on the effects of attractiveness on political candidates. She asked 125 undergraduate students to rank two groups of photographs, one of men and one of women, in order of attractiveness. The students were told the photographs were of candidates for political offices. They were asked to rank them again, in the order they would vote for them.

The results showed that attractive males utterly defeated unattractive men, but the women who had been ranked most attractive invariably received the fewest votes.

26. The word "liability" (Line 4, Para. 1) most probably means "_____".

A. misfortune   B. instability   C. disadvantage   D. burden

27. In traditionally female jobs, attractiveness _____.

A. reinforces the feminine qualities required

B. makes women look more honest and capable

C. is of primary importance to women

D. often enables women to succeed quickly

28. Bowman's experiment reveals that when it comes to politics, attractiveness _____.

A. turns out to be an obstacle to men

B. affects men and women alike

C. has as little effect on men as on women

D. is more of an obstacle than a benefit to women

29. It can be inferred from the passage that people's views on beauty are often _____.

A. practical   B. prejudiced   C. old-fashioned   D. radical

30. The author writes this passage to _____.

A. discuss the negative aspects of being attractive
B. give advice to job-seekers who are attractive
C. demand equal rights for women
D. emphasize the importance of appearance

Model Test 4

Part I Reading Comprehension (Skimming and Scanning) (15 minutes)

Directions: *In this part, you will have 15 minutes to go over the passage quickly and answer the questions on* **Answer Sheet 1** *.*

For questions 1 ~ 7, mark

Y (*for YES*)   *if the statement agrees with the information given in the passage;*

N (*for NO*)   *if the statement contradicts the information given in the passage;*

NG (*for NOT GIVEN*)   *if the information is not given in the passage.*

For questions 8 ~ 10, complete the sentences with the information given in the passage.

Improving Your T.Q. (Test-Taking Quotient)

You will have one hour to complete this test. All answers must be marked on the answer sheet. Make no marks on the test booklet. Using a No.2 pencil, place your name... Ready? Begin.

They are off ~ ! Each test-taker working at a different pace; each using a different technique and strategy; all wishing they were somewhere else.

Ours is a test-taking culture. And whether you are an adult job-hunter, license-applicant or student, tests always provoke uncertainty, especially if life decisions are attached to them.

In 12 years of your elementary and secondary education, you completed a conservative estimate of 2,600 weekly quizzes: college mid-term and final examinations over a four-year period account for another 100, and each year of advanced professional training adds another 25 major exams.

People do not realize that classroom examinations represent only a small segment of testing experience. School systems administer approximately 2 million standardized tests in addition to regular classroom tests.

The total number administered by business, government, industry and clinics, however, is *astronomical*(庞大无法估计的), dwarfing the total number of school tests.

People tend to take tests without really understanding them. One sure way to improve your performance is to familiarize yourself with the different types of examinations. Simply understanding the test format promotes self-confidence.

Can familiarity with test-taking boost you test score? Yes, along with 15 other "tricks". Read on.

All tests—whether simple classroom quizzes, tests for a driver's license of statistically oriented aptitude test—have one major point in common: A test is a measure of a person's behavior at on point in time.

A long-held myth has led most people to conclude that test scores are forever. This is simply not true.

Scores change from on test-taking to the next. In fact, there are numerous reported cases of intelligence quotients(IQs) *fluctuating*(变动) as much as 30 or 40 points between test administrations.

Another source of score fluctuation is a result of the test-taker's uncertainty with different types of tests.

Overall there are two specific types: maximal- and typical-performance tests. Maximal tests attempt to measure an individual's best possible performance accurately. Included in this type are intelligence tests, academic or classroom (achievement) tests and aptitude tests. Of these, IQ tests are the most widely known and the least understood.

It's amazing how so much confusion over those two little letters > IQ, has *proliferated*(扩散) since the testing movement began in the early 1900s. The first intelligence tests were conceived by Alfred Binet, a French psychologist, who was asked to develop a procedure to predict which children were unable to learn in classroom setting. Today there are approximately 350 intelligence tests on the market.

Myths surrounding the IQ test have grossly contaminated the public's understanding; people want the IQ test to do more than it is capable of doing. It is best used to predict school success: to assess mental skills and the ability to adapt in new situations and learn academically.

Another maximal-performance test is an admissions test (technically a form of aptitude testing). These tests are designed to measure the degree of skill of people when they are attempting to perform to the limit of their ability. But people allow these tests to intimidate them, and that puts them under a great deal tension. If you've taken one of these exams previously, chances are your score will increase in subsequent testing.

Two important pints her: First, put the practice rule to work for you (familiarity, again). Second, ask friends who have taken the test what they remember about it, and then check your local bookstore for manuals that will prepare you for the test. Books currently on the market that raise scores do so not by divulging knowledge, but by giving you familiarity with the items and test formats.

Typical performance tests do not promote as much anxiety as maximal-performance tests, for they are designed to assess interests, personality traits, attitudes and other similar characteristics. There is little preparation needed and no "right" or "wrong" answers.

Now for the 15 other tricks:

1. When it is possible to prepare for a test, do so! In fact, "over-learn" the material.

Research consistently shows that over-learning the material reduces anxiety and raises test scores.

Also, it has been found that consistent studying over a period of time is more effective than cramming just before a test. Going to the movies the night before an exam can be *therapeutic*(有效果的). How do you know when over-learning takes place? When you feel you have mastered the subject, study one or two hours more.

2. Show up on time, but not early. If you must get there early, stand alone, away from the crowd. If you pay attention to other's worries, your anxiety level will increase, too.

3. Know in advance if the test has a correction formula. For example, for every four items you answer incorrectly, one right one might be deducted from your total score. If you answer 50 items correctly, but miss 20, after the correction formula, your score would be 45.

4. Eliminate alternatives. If the item is a four-choice, multiple-choice format, the odds are one in four you could guess the right one. If you can eliminate any tow of the four, your odds are 50 – 50. If you cannot eliminate any of the alternatives, you have no idea which one is correct, and if there is no correction for guessing, then pick the longest answer and proceed to the next test question.

Test authors tend to make the correct answer the longest.

5. Test authors also tend to make one of two parallel statements the correct answer. For instance, if two of the four choices have major differences in wording; and if the other two are almost identical in structure and wording, chances are one of the parallel statements is right.

Probably the longer statement will get you points.

6. Read directions carefully. Many points are lost because people don't understand what they are supposed to do.

7. If the test if multiple-choice, requiring you to read a "stem" and then select one correct response from four alternatives, attempt to answer the question before you read the possible choices. After you formulate your answer, match your ideas to the possibilities and pick the one most similar. By doing this, you are using not only recognition but recall.

8. Pace yourself so you complete as many items as possible. Sometimes the items at the end of a test are weighted more because fewer people answer them.

9. If the test requires you to read long passages and then answer questions about the reading, read the questions first. By doing this, you will know what you are looking for as you read, and you'll be in a much better position to answer. If the test is timed, this technique

also increases your speed and efficiency.

10. Skip items you are unsure of, items about material you've seen before but can't remember the answer immediately. Chances are your brain will be searching for and *retrieving* (重新得到) the information while you are working on other items. When the answer comes to you, go back and mark it.

11. Do not change your answers on multiple-choice tests unless you are very uncertain about your initial answer. Research has shown that only when you have strong doubts is your second answer more likely to be correct.

12. Read the questions carefully. On essay tests, note such key words as compare, contrast, discuss, evaluate, analyze, define and describe. If you are unsure about an essay question, your response will come across as wordiness. Do what the question asks, be direct, make your point and support it. On multiple-choice tests, look out for such negative disclaimers as, "Which of the following could not be...?"

As you read the test questions, underline the key words. This will recheck your thinking.

13. There is some evidence that if you are slightly cool you will do better on a test. Informal observations certainly support this point. For instance, if your are too warm, you may become sleepy and lose your focus.

14. Re-check your work. Make clerical corrections only.

15. Finally, ask to see your corrected test and scores. By reviewing a test, you become test-wise.

Tests are necessary to determine levels of knowledge and to help make placement decisions. They are capable of motivating via feedback. So it is important to develop a healthy, positive attitude toward examinations.

As tests are mastered they serve as "trial runs" for other, more difficult life tests.

1. There are altogether about 100 mid-term and final exams over a four year period of college education.

2. The total number of tests held by government, business and industry, etc. is much bigger than those held by schools.

3. Maximal performance tests promote less anxiety than typical performance test.

4. If you get early for the test, you should stand alone and go over your material.

5. If there is no correction for guessing, then pick the shortest answer and proceed to the next test question.

6. If you are not sure of an item, you just simply go to the next item and come back to it later when you recall the information of it.

7. It is shown that if you are slightly cool you won't do better on a test.

8. _____ attempt to measure an individual's best possible performance accurately.

9. Another maximal-performance test is an _____ (technically a form of aptitude testing).

10. Tests are _____ to determine levels of knowledge and to help make placement decisions.

Part II Reading Comprehension (Reading in Depth) (25 minutes)

Section A

Directions: *In this section, there is a passage with ten blanks. You are required to select one word for each blank from a list of choices given in a word bank following the passage. Read the passage through carefully before making your choices. Each choice in bank is identified by a letter. Please mark the corresponding letter for each item on* **Answer Sheet 2** *with a single line through the center.* **You may not use any of the words in the bank more than once.**

Questions 11 to 20 are based on the following passage.

In 776 BC, the first Olympic games were held at the foot of Mount Olympus to __11__ the Greeks' chief god, Zeus. The Greeks emphasized __12__ fitness and strength in their education of youth. Therefore, __13__ in running, jumping, discus and javelin throwing, boxing, and horse and chariot racing were held in __14__ cities. The __15__ competed every four years at Mount Olympus. The winners were __16__ honored by having olive wreaths placed on their heads and having poems sung about their deeds. __17__ , these were held as games of friendship, and any wars in __18__ were stopped to allow the games to take place.

The Greeks __19__ so much importance to these games that they calculated time in four year __20__ called "Olympiads" dating from 776 BC.

A. remember	I. sportsman
B. greatly	J. participants
C. contests	K. physical
D. attached	L. mental
E. honor	M. individual
F. cycles	N. Originally
G. progress	O. specially
H. period	

Section B

Directions: *There are 2 passages in this section. Each passage is followed by some questions or unfinished statement. For each of them there are four choices marked A, B, C and D. You should decide on the best choice and mark the corresponding letter on* **Answer Sheet 2** *with a single line through the center.*

Passage One

Questions 21 to 25 are based on the following passage.

Except for the Indians, the earliest backpackers in America were frontiersmen, who roamed the wilderness looking either for necessities such as food and water or for sources of wealth such as fur and gold. For them backpacking was a way of survival or a means of achieving what one day would be called the "American Dream". Today, however, many people enjoy backpacking as a recreational activity. Shouldering a pack and leaving behind the world of telephone, television, and traffic promise an exciting experience. Testing one's **stamina** (耐力) and skills are challenging a sense of one's place in the natural world can be rewarding. Moreover, backpacking is an activity that can last any length for time and can be enjoyed alone or with friends. Then too, a backpacking trip may be organized within a day or two. The backpacker and his friends have only to decide on their destination and then organize the all-important kit, whose contents they must depend on throughout their trip. A map, a compass, a flashlight, along with first aid equipment, food, and extra clothing can be rounded up without much difficulty. Once the backpackers have left word about where they go in a note on the refrigerator door or in a message on an answering machine, they can look forward to an adventure that will lit the spirit and nourish the soul. Their outing will enable them to return in a short time to the age of technology with the courage and independence of Natty Bumppo, who did indeed belong to the age of the frontier.

21. The passage mainly discusses _____.

A. the early backpackers

B. backpacking as a perfect form of recreation

C. how backpacking started

D. why people of today are interested in backpacking

22. The earliest backpackers were _____.

A. frontiersmen   B. Indians   C. fur traders   D. gold miners

23. Early backpackers who roamed about in wilderness were interested in finding _____.

A. means to realize the American dream   B. recreation in life

C. relief form the stress of everyday life   D. daily necessities

24. One of the advantages of backpacking is that _____.

A. it can help people to establish a link with nature

B. it is a group activity and can cure a person's loneliness

C. it is not so challenging as other activities

D. it does not require people to decide on a destination

25. According to the passage, Natty Bumppo was _____.

A. an American national hero   B. a character in a Hemingway novel

C. a man of valor   D. an Indian warrior

Passage Two

Questions 26 to 30 are based on the following passage.

They are among the 250,000 people under the age of 25 who are out of work in the Netherlands, a group that accounts for 40 percent of the nation's unemployed. A storm of anger boiled up at the government-sponsored youth center, even among those who are continuing their studies.

"We study for jobs that don't exist." Nicollete Steggerda, 23, said.

After three decades of prosperity, unemployment among 10 member nations of the European Community has exceeded 11 percent, affecting a total of 12.3 million people, and the number is climbing.

The bitter disappointment long expressed by British youths is spreading across the Continent. The title of a rock song "No Future" can now be seen written on the brick walls of closed factories in Belgium and France.

Recent surveys have found that the increasing argument in the last few years over the deployment in Europe of North Atlantic Treaty Organization missiles and the possibility of nuclear war have clouded European youths' confidence in the future.

One form of protest tends to put the responsibility for a country's economic troubles on the large numbers of "guest workers" from Third World nations, people welcomed in Western Europe in the years of prosperity.

Young Europeans, brought up in an extended period of economic success and general stability seem to resemble Americans more than they do their own parents. Material enjoyment has given them a sense of expectation, even the right, to a standard of living that they see around them.

"And so we pass the days at the discos, or meet people at the café, and sit and stare," said Isabella Gault. "There is usually not much conversation. You look for happiness. Sometimes you even find it."

26. Unemployment in the Netherlands has affected _____.

A. one million people   B. roughly 0.6 million people

C. 250,000 people   D. less than half of the population

27. What Nicollete Steggerda said (Para. 2) means that _____.

A. school education is not sufficient

B. what the students learn is more than necessary

C. the students cannot get work after graduation

D. the students' aim in study is not clear

28. The word "prosperity" (Para.6, Line 4) most probably means _____.

A. achievements in economy   B. advance in politics
C. economic troubles   D. political crisis

29. Which of the following statements is NOT true?

A. The rock song "No Future" is an expression of the disappointment of European youth.

B. 40% of the guest workers are out of work in Western Europe now.

C. European youths are worried about a new world war in the future.

D. Widespread unemployment is beyond European youths' expectation.

30. British youths _____.

A. are trying to find work on the Continent

B. are sympathetic with the unemployed on the Continent

C. have been the first to show their disappointment over joblessness

D. show their concern for unemployment in France and Belgiu

Model Test 5

Part I Reading Comprehension

Part I **Reading Comprehension**（**Skimming and Scanning**）（**15 minutes**）

Directions: *In this part, you will have 15 minutes to go over the passage quickly and answer the questions on **Answer Sheet** 1.*

For questions 1 ~ 7, mark

Y（*for YES*）   *if the statement agrees with the information given in the passage;*

N（*for NO*）   *if the statement contradicts the information given in the passage;*

NG（*for NOT GIVEN*）   *if the information is not given in the passage.*

For questions 8 ~ 10, complete the sentences with the information given in the passage.

The dog

The dog is one of the most popular pets in the world. It ordinarily remains loyal to a considerate master, and because of this the dog has been called man's best friend. Class distinctions between people have no part in a dog's life. It can be a faithful companion to either rich or poor.

Man's Best Friend

Dogs have been domesticated for most of human history and have thus endeared themselves to many over the years. Stories have been told about brave dogs that served admirably in war or that risked their lives to save persons in danger. When Pompeli— the Roman community destroyed by Mount Vesuvius in AD 79— was finally *excavated* （挖掘）, searchers found evidence of a dog lying across a child, apparently trying to protect the youngster. Perhaps few of the millions of dogs in the world may be so heroic, but they are still a source of genuine delight to their owners.

A dog fits easily into family life. It thrives on praise and affection. When a master tells a dog that it is good, the animal happily wags its tail. But when a master scolds a dog, it *skulks* （躲闪） away with a sheepish look and with its tail tucked between its legs.

People in the city as well as those in other areas can enjoy a dog. Medium-size or small dogs are best suited for the confines of the city. Large dogs need considerable exercise over a large area.

Dogs are not always well thought of, however. In recent years dogs in the city have been

31

in the center of controversy. Some people have criticized dog owners for allowing their pets to soil sidewalks and lawns, although in some cities laws oblige owners to walk their dogs along street curbs. In turn, dog owners have argued that the animals serve as protection against vandals and burglars and thus protect their detractors as well as their owner.

When a person decides to own a dog, he should be prepared to care for it properly. For a dog to stay healthy it must be correctly fed and adequately groomed, and its medical needs must be met. For a dog to be well-mannered it must be properly trained. It should never be ill-treated or mishandled. Otherwise, it will bite in its own defense.

The Dog Family

The wild ancestors of all dogs were hunters. Wolves and other wild relatives of the dog still hunt in packs for their food. Dogs have retained the urge to be with the pack. This is why they do not like to be left alone for long. Some breeds of dogs still retain the hunting instinct.

Dogs exist in a wide range of sexes, colors, and temperaments. Some, such as the Doberman pinscher and German shepherd, serve as alert and aggressive watchdogs. Others, such as the beagle and cocker spaniel, are playful family pets, even though they were bred for hunting. Still others, such as the collie and the Welsh corgi, can herd farm or range animals. Each of the dogs just mentioned is a purebred. A mongrel dog, however—one with many breeds in its background—can just as easily fit into family life.

Dogs have been with humans since prehistoric times. Over the years they have performed various services. They have pulled sleds over snowy tracts. They have delivered messages, herded sheep and cattle, and even rescued persons trapped in the snow. Dogs have served as a source of food, too. The ancient Romans are said to have prized certain kinds of dog stew. The Aztecs of ancient Mexico raise tiny dogs, thought to be the forebears of the Chihuahua, to feed the large carnivores(食肉动物) in the private zoos of the Aztec rulers. In the past dogs have even been worshiped as gods. Recently, they have been used in drug research, medical experimentation, and space science. Soviet scientists launched dogs into space to test the ability of mammals to survive the harshness of space travel before people were sent up.

Dog Training

Dogs are trained as guard dogs in peacetime by the United States Army and other military services. Because of their keen sense of smell, dogs are used by police at times to track down escaped prisoners. Law enforcement agencies also rely on the dog's acute sense of smell to uncover illegal drugs. And specially trained dogs serve as the "eyes" of the blind, guiding the steps of their sightless masters around obstacles and hazards.

Any young dog can be trained to understand commands and to do simple tricks. When correctly trained, it is conditioned to respond to your commands, noises, or gestures.

Once an owner decides to train his puppy, however, he must be willing to stick with the hob until the puppy learns the task. First, the owner should select a simple "call" name for the animal. The call name should be used frequently so the puppy can learn to recognize the sound of it.

A training session is best begun when the puppy is hungry because it is more alert at that time. Also, the owner can reinforce the dog's correct responses to commands with a dog biscuit or meat *tidbit*(少量的精美事物). The hungry dog is more apt to associate the correct performance of a task with a food reward.

To get the puppy into a collar at first, entice it to you by extending your open hands, pet it and say "good dog" (and include its name) when it comes, and finally slip the collar around its neck. Then attach a leash to the collar. If the puppy has confidence in you, it will walk along with you even though it is wearing the leash. A metal chain leash is usually best because the puppy will not be able to chew and play with it.

Wait until a puppy is at least six months old before trying to teach it tricks, but do teach it the meaning of "no" at an earlier age. The young dog must be corrected vocally each time it does something that you disapprove of. If you are consistent, it soon learns by your tone of voice what pleases you and what displeases you. Formal training sessions should entail no more than ten minutes of work at a time, and they should never tire the dog.

To teach the command "sit", keep the dog on your left side and pull up on its leash with your right hand while gently but firmly pushing its hindquarters to the floor. While doing this, say the command "sit" with authority. Reinforces its correct actions with a tidbit.

To teach the command "stay", work with the puppy after it has learned to sit. While it is sitting, raise your palm to the dog and order it to "stay". It will probably try to get up, so tell it "no". Whenever it remains in the sitting position after you have given the "stay" command, reward the dog with a tidbit.

More effort might be needed to teach the command "come". When the dog has learned to stay, command it to "come" and call it by bane. When it comes to you, lavish the dog with praise and give it a snack. A very stubborn dog might have to be pulled with a cord tied around its collar while the command is given. If this is necessary, be firm but accompany the command with a friendly hand gesture. Many tugs may be necessary until the reluctant dog learns the meaning of "come". Do not be impatient with a puppy when teaching it simple tricks, and never get angry. If the training sessions are not going well, break them off and resume them later in the day or even on another day. In addition, give praise and tidbits to the dog only when they are earned.

1. The dogs are faithful to their owners, regardless of their class distinctions.
2. Because of their loyalty to their owners, the dogs have won completely welcome from all

people in recent years.

3. Although many dogs are kept alone, they prefer to stay within a group of dogs.

4. Dogs are able to help human beings by taking care of children.

5. The best time for a training session to begin is when the dog is somewhat hungry because the trainer can use food to tempt the dog to follow his command.

6. The dog owners should teach their dogs the meaning of "no" at an early age with a hand gesture.

7. When the training sessions do not go well, the trainers should be firm and give the command more strictly.

8. Dogs have been with humans since _____ times.

9. Dogs are trained as _____ in peacetime by the United States Army and other military services.

10. To teach the command "stay", work with the puppy _____ it has learned to sit.

Part II Reading Comprehension (Reading in Depth) (25 minutes)
Section A

Directions: *In this section, there is a passage with ten blanks. You are required to select one word for each blank from a list of choices given in a word bank following the passage. Read the passage through carefully before making your choices. Each choice in bank is identified by a letter. Please mark the corresponding letter for each item on **Answer Sheet 2** with a single line through the center. **You may not use any of the words in the bank more than once.***

Questions 11 to 20 are based on the following passage.

It may seem strange to think that a plant could actually ___11___ the course of human history, but wheat has been ___12___ important to people for thousands of years. Long ago, when it was discovered that wheat could be cultivated, the living ___13___ of our ancestors changed. At one time, they had been forced to roam the forests and plains of the Earth in ___14___ of wild game and ___15___ plants. But when people discovered that wheat could be ___16___, they were able to build ___17___ and to farm their wheat nearby. Wheat was a kind of food that could be grown fairly easily, then ___18___ and stored for use during the winter months. Wheat, probably ___19___ than any other food, made the beginning of ___20___ possible.

A. culture	I. manners
B. cultivated	J. more
C. affect	K. search
D. habits	L. civilization
E. harvested	M. vitally
F. edible	N. houses
G. influence	O. settlements
H. rather	

Section B

Directions: *There are 2 passages in this section. Each passage is followed by some questions or unfinished statement. For each of them there are four choices marked A, B, C and D. You should decide on the best choice and mark the corresponding letter on* **Answer Sheet 2** *with a single line through the center.*

Passage One

Questions 21 to 25 are based on the following passage.

One phase of the business cycle is the expansion phase. This phase is a two-fold one, including recovery and prosperity. During the recovery period there is ever-growing expansion of existing facilities and new facilities for production are created. More businesses are created and older ones expanded. Improvements of various kinds are made. There is an ever increasing optimism about the future of economic growth. Much capital is invested in machinery or heavy industry. More labor is employed. More raw materials are required. As one part of the economy develops, other parts are affected. For example, a great expansion in automobiles results in an expansion of the steel glass, and rubber industries. Roads are required, thus the cement and machinery industries are stimulated. Demand for labor and materials results in greater prosperity for workers and suppliers of raw materials, including farmers. This increases purchasing power and the volume of goods bought and sold. Thus prosperity is diffused among the various segments of the population. This prosperity period may continue to rise and rise without an apparent end. However, a time comes when this phase reaches a peak and stops spiraling upwards. This is the ending of the expansion phase.

21. We may assume that in the next paragraph the writer will discuss _____.

A. cyclical industries   B. the status of the farmer

C. the higher cost of living   D. the recession period

22. The title below that best expresses the ideas of this passage is _____.

A. The Business Cycle   B. The Recovery Stage

C. An Expanding Society   D. The Period of Good Times

23. Prosperity in one industry _____.

A. reflects itself in many other industries

B. will spiral upwards

C. will affect the steel industry

D. will end abruptly

24. Which of the following industries will probably be a good indicator of a period of expansion?

A. Toys.   B. Machine tools.   C. Foodstuffs.   D. Farming.

25. During the period of prosperity, people regard the future _____ .

A. cautiously   B. in a confident manner

C. opportunity   D. indifferently

Passage Two

Questions 26 to 30 are based on the following passage.

The Ordinance of 1784 is most significant historically because it embodied the principle that new states should be formed from the western region and admitted to the Union on an equal basis with the original commonwealths. This principle, which underlay the whole later development of the continental United States, was generally accepted by this time and cannot be properly credited to an single man. Thomas Jefferson had presented precisely this idea to his own state of Virginia before the Declaration of Independence, however, and if he did not originate it he was certainly one of those who held it first. It had been basic in his own thinking about the future of the Republic throughout the struggle for independence. He had no desire to break from the British Empire simply to establish an American one — in which the newer region should be subsidiary and tributary to the old. What he dreamed of was an expanding union of self-governing commonwealths, joined as a group of peers.

26. Which of the following proposals did the ordinance of 1784 incorporate?

A. New states should be admitted to the Union in numbers equal to the older states.

B. The Union should make the western region into tributary states.

C. New states should share the same rights in the Union as the original states.

D. The great western region should be divided into twelve states.

27. According to the passage, what was the general attitude toward the principle underlying the Ordinance of 1784?

A. It was considered the most important doctrine of the day.

B. It received wide support at that time.

C. It was more popular in Virginia than elsewhere.

D. It was thought to be original and creative.

28. According to the passage, one of Thomas Jefferson's political goals was to _____ .

A. maintain strong ties with the British Empire

B. fight for more territory for his country

C. found the Republican Party

D. guarantee the status of new states

29. The author implies which of the following happened to new lands that became part of the British Empire?

A. They were not considered equal to Britain itself.

B. They established a separate empire of their own.

C. They had an equal share in the government of the empire.

D. They were ruled by a group of peers.

30. The paragraph following this passage most probably would discuss _____.

A. Jefferson's home in eastern Virginia

B. the implementation of the Ordinance of 1784

C. British colonial expansion outside North America

D. the economic development of Virginia

Model Test 6

Part I Reading Comprehension (Skimming and Scanning) (15 minutes)

Directions: *In this part, you will have 15 minutes to go over the passage quickly and answer the questions on **Answer Sheet 1**.*

For questions 1 ~ 7, mark

Y (*for YES*)   *if the statement agrees with the information given in the passage;*

N (*for NO*)   *if the statement contradicts the information given in the passage;*

NG (*for NOT GIVEN*)   *if the information is not given in the passage.*

For questions 8 ~ 10, complete the sentences with the information given in the passage.

The Teacher Changed His Life

Steve, a twelve-year-old boy with alcoholic parents, was about to be lost forever, by the U.S. education system. Remarkably, he could read, yet, in spite of his reading skills, Steve was failing. He had been failing since first grade, as he was passed on from grade to grade. Steve was a big boy, looking more like a teenager than a twelve-year-old; yet, Steve went unnoticed... until Miss White.

Miss White was a smiling, young, beautiful red hair, and Steve was in love! For the first time in his young life, he couldn't take his eyes off his teacher; yet, still he failed. He never did his homework, and he was always in trouble with Miss White. His heart would break under her sharp words, and when he was punished for failing to turn in his homework, he felt just miserable! Still, he did not study.

In the middle of the first semester of school, the entire seventh grade was tested for basic skills. Steve hurried through his tests, and continued to dream of other things, as the day wore on. His heart was not in school, but in the woods, where he often escaped alone, trying to shut out the sights, sounds and smells of his alcoholic home. No one checked on him to see if he was safe. No one knew he was gone, because no one was sober enough to care. Oddly, Steve never missed a day of school.

One day, Miss White's impatient voice broke into his daydreams.

"Steve!!" Startled, he turned to look at her.

"Pay attention!"

Steve locked his gaze on Miss White with adolescent adoration, as she began to go over the test results for the seventh grade.

"You all did pretty well," she told the class, "except for one boy, and it breaks my heart to tell you this, but..." She hesitated, pinning Steve to his seat with a sharp stare, her eyes searching his face.

"The smartest boy in the seventh grade is failing my class!"

She just stared at Steve, as the class spun around for a good look. Steve dropped his eyes and carefully examined his fingertips.

After that, it was war!! Steve still wouldn't do his homework. Even as the punishments became more severe, he remained stubborn.

"Just try it! ONE WEEK!" He was unmoved.

"You're smart enough! You'll see a change!" Nothing fazed him.

"Give yourself a chance! Don't give up on your life!"

"Steve! Please! I care about you!"

Wow! Suddenly, Steve got it!! Someone cared about him? Someone, totally unattainable and perfect, CARED ABOUT HIM??!!

Steve went home from school, thoughtful, that afternoon. Walking into the house, he took one look around. Both parents were passed out, in various stages of undress, and the stench was overpowering! He, quickly, gathered up his camping gear, a jar of peanut butter, a loaf of bread, a bottle of water, and this time... his schoolbooks. Grim faced and determined, he headed for the woods.

The following Monday he arrived at school on time, and he waited for Miss White to enter the classroom. She walked in, all sparkle and smiles! God, she was beautiful! He yearned for her smile to turn on him. It did not.

Miss White, immediately, gave a quiz on the weekend homework. Steve hurried through the test, and was the first to hand in his paper. With a look of surprise, Miss White took his paper. Obviously puzzled, she began to look it over. Steve walked back to his desk, his heart pounding within his chest. As he sat down, he couldn't resist another look at the lovely woman.

Miss White's face was in total shock! She glanced up at Steve, then down, then up.

Suddenly, her face broke into a radiant smile. The smartest boy in the seventh grade had just passed his first test!

From that moment nothing was the same for Steve. Life at home remained the same, but life still changed. He discovered that not only could he learn, but he was good at it!

He discovered that he could understand and retain knowledge, and that he could translate the things he learned into his own life. Steve began to excel! And he continued this course throughout his school life.

After high-school Steve enlisted in the Navy, and he had a successful military career. During that time, he met the love of his life, he raised a family, and he graduated from college Magna Cum Laude. During his Naval career, he inspired many young people, who without him, might not have believed in themselves. Steve began a second career after the Navy, and he continues to inspire others, as an adjunct professor in a nearby college Miss White left a great legacy. She saved one boy who has changed many lives.

You see, it's simple, really. A change took place within the heart of one boy, all because of one teacher, who cared.

1. Since Steven had alcoholic parents, he didn't like to study.
2. Steven liked Miss White, for she was beautiful.
3. Miss White was disappointed when she found Steven didn't pass the exam.
4. In Miss White's eye, Steven was a stupid student.
5. Miss White changed Steven's school life and family life.
6. Steven became the excellent soldier in the Navy.
7. Steven began his second career as an adjunct professor.
8. After Miss White found Steven passed the test, her face broke into _____.
9. He discovered that he could understand and retain knowledge, _____.
10. During his Naval career, he inspired many young people, who without him, _____.

Part II Reading Comprehension (Reading in Depth) (25 minutes)
Section A
Directions: *In this section, there is a passage with ten blanks. You are required to select one word for each blank from a list of choices given in a word bank following the passage. Read the passage through carefully before making your choices. Each choice in bank is identified by a letter. Please mark the corresponding letter for each item on **Answer Sheet 2** with a single line through the center. **You may not use any of the words in the bank more than once**.*
Questions 11 to 20 are based on the following passage.

Tennis hopeful Jamie Hunt, 16, felt he could not become a world-class junior player while attending a regular school. The international circuit has players on the road 50% of the time—and it's hard to focus on your backhand when you're worrying about being on time for homeroom. So last year Hunt, who hones his ground strokes at Elite TNT Tennis Academy in April Sound, Texas, enrolled for academics in the $9,750-a-year University of Miami Online High School (UMOHS), a virtual school that __11__ to athletes. "The online school gives me the flexibility I need," says Hunt. "The workload is the same, but I can do it anywhere. It's nicer to ask a question face-to-face with a teacher, but in some ways it prepares me better for college because I have to be more ___12___ ." A year ago, Hunt's world junior ranking was 886; now it's 108.

Virtual high schools, which allow students to take classes via PC, have emerged as an increasingly popular education alternative, particularly for ___13___ athletes. UMOHS has more than 400 students enrolled, 65% of whom are athletes. ___14___ by the 100-year-old Southern Association of Colleges and Schools, UMOHS offers honors and advanced-placement classes. All course material is online, along with ___15___ and due dates. For help, says Principal Howard Liebman, "a student may E-mail, instant message or call the teacher."

Dallas mom Lori Bannon turned to another online school, Laurel Springs in Ojai, Calif. Bannon, who has a medical degree from Harvard, didn't want to ___16___ the education of her daughter Lindsay, 13, an élite gymnast who spends eight hours a day in the gym. "Regular school was not an ___17___ ," says Bannon, "but I wanted to make sure she could go back at grade level if she quit gymnastics." Laurel Springs' ___18___ has increased 35% a year for the past four years, to 1,800 students. At least 25% are either athletes or child entertainers.

Educators are split on the merits of such schools. Paul Orehovec, an enrollment officer for the University of Miami, admits, "I was somewhat of a ___19___ . But when I looked into their programs and accreditation, I was excited. UMOHS is the first online school to be granted membership in the National Honor Society." Kevin Roy, Elite's director of education, sees pitfalls and potential in virtual schools. "You will never have that wonderful teacher who ___20___ you for life," says Roy. "But the virtual school offers endless possibilities. I don't know where education's imagination will take this."

A. caters	I. assignments
B. never	J. option
C. skeptic	K. on-the-go
D. admits	L. online
E. inspires	M. Accredited
F. independent	N. enrollment
G. compromise	O. Virtual
H. possibilities	

Section B

Directions: *There are 2 passages in this section. Each passage is followed by some questions or unfinished statements. For each of them are four choices marked A, B, C and D. You should decide on the best choice and mark the corresponding letter on **Answer Sheet 2** with a single line through the centre.*

41

Passage One

Questions 21 to 25 are based on the following passage.

Carly Fiorina, Hewlett-Packard's chief executive, came out fighting on November 14th. In a conference call with analysts, she announced better-than-expected quarterly results, even though profits were down. Ms Fiorina also reiterated why she believes her $ 24 billion plan to acquire Compaq is the best way forward for HP, despite objections by Hewlett and Packard family members. Last week Walter Hewlett, whose father co-founded the company, expressed concern that the merger would increase HP's exposure to the shrinking PC market and would distract managers from the more important task of navigating through the recession.

There are two ways to defend the deal. One is to point out its advantages, which is what Ms Fiorina did this week. Merging with Compaq, she said, would enable HP to reach its goals faster than it could on its own. The deal would improve HP's position in key markets such as storage and high-end computing, as well as the economics of its PC business. It would double the size of HP's sales force and broaden its customer base, providing more potential clients for its services and consulting arms. It would improve cashflow, margins and efficiency by adding "breadth and depth" to HP. "Having spent the last several months planning the integration of these two companies, we are even more convinced of the power of this combination," Ms Fiorina concluded.

It sounds too good to be true, and it almost certainly is. But the other way to defend the deal is to point out that, even if it was a bad idea to start with, abandoning it could be even worse—a view that, unsurprisingly, Ms Fiorina chose not to advance, but is being quietly put forward by the deal's supporters.

Scrapping the merger would be extremely painful for a number of reasons. Since the executive teams of both firms have committed themselves to the deal, they would be utterly discredited if it fell apart, and would probably have to go. Under the terms of the merger agreement, HP might have to pay Compaq as much as $ 675 m if it backed out. The two firms would be considerably weakened; they would also be rivals again, despite having shared confidential technical and marketing information with each other over the past few months. In short, it would all be horribly messy. What can be done to save the deal? Part of the problem is that HP has no plan B. "They need a brand-recovery effort immediately," says one industry analyst. HP must give the impression that it is strong and vital, rather than desperate, and that its future is not dependent on the deal going forward. That could make the merger look more attractive and bring investors back on board.

This week's results will certainly help. The David and Lucile Packard Foundation, which owns just over one-tenth of HP's shares, will decide whether to back the merger in the next few weeks, and HP's shareholders are to vote on it early next year. The more credible HP's plan

B, the less likely it is that it will be needed.

21. What is Ms Fiorina's attitude toward the merging of HP and Compaq?

A. Slight contempt.   B. Strong disappointed.

C. Enthusiastic support.   D. Reserved consent.

22. Which of the following is not the good reason to promote the merger?

A. The majority of the firm are in favor of the merger.

B. No combination is even worse than merger.

C. It can bring about a lot of advantages.

D. There is no plan B to save the firm from trouble.

23. The expression "The more credible HP's plan B, the less likely it is that it will be needed."(Last Line, Last Paragraph) most probably indicates _____.

A. the reliance on plan B determines the success of the merger

B. the merger needs people's trust in plan B

C. plan B can win people's trust

D. appearing not to be dependent on the merger will make the merger go well

24. What can we learn from paragraph 4?

A. The executive teams of both firms can benefit a lot from the merger.

B. The future of HP depends much on the merger.

C. The two sides are eager to make this deal.

D. Plan B can save HP out of trouble.

25. What is the author's attitude toward the merger of HP?

A. Negative.   B. Apprehensive.   C. Objective.   D. Supportive.

Passage Two

Questions 26 to 30 are based on the following passage.

By almost every measure, Paul Pfingst is an unsentimental prosecutor. Last week the San
Diego County district attorney said he fully intends to try suspect Charles Andrew Williams,
15, as an adult for the Santana High School shootings. Even before the tragedy, Pfingst had
stood behind the controversial California law that mandates treating murder suspects as young as
14 as adults.

So nobody would have wagered that Pfingst would also be the first D.A. in the U.S. to
launch his very own Innocence Project. Yet last June, Pfingst told his attorneys to go back over
old murder and rape convictions and see if any unravel with newly developed DNA-testing
tools. In other words, he wanted to revisit past victories—this time playing for the other team.
"I think people misunderstand being conservative for being biased," says Pfingst. "I consider
myself a pragmatic guy, and I have no interest in putting innocent people in jail."

Around the U.S., flabbergasted defense attorneys and their jailed clients cheered his move. Among prosecutors, however, there was an awkward pause. After all, each DNA test costs as much as $5,000. Then there's the unspoken risk: if dozens of innocents turn up, the D.A. will have indicted his shop.

But nine months later, no budgets have been busted or prosecutors ousted. Only the rare case merits review. Pfingst's team considers convictions before 1993, when the city started routine DNA testing. They discard cases if the defendant has been released. Of the 560 remaining files, they have re-examined 200, looking for cases with biological evidence and defendants who still claim innocence.

They have identified three so far. The most compelling involves a man serving 12 years for molesting a girl who was playing in his apartment. But others were there at the time. Police found a small drop of saliva on the victim's shirt—too small a sample to test in 1991. Today that spot could free a man. Test results are due any day. Inspired by San Diego, 10 other counties in the U.S. are starting DNA audits.

26. How did Pfingst carry out his own Innocence Project?

A. By his cooperation with his attorneys.

B. By revisiting the past victories.

C. By using the newly developed DNA-testing tools.

D. By getting rid of his bias against the suspects.

27. Which of the following can be an advantage of Innocence Project?

A. To help correct the wrong judgments.

B. To trust the unqualified prosecutors.

C. To trap the prosecutors in an awkward situation.

D. To cheer up the defense attorneys and their jailed clients.

28. The expression "flabbergasted" (Line 1, Paragraph 3) most probably means _____.

A. excited   B. competent   C. embarrassed   D. astounded

29. Why was Pfingst an unsentimental prosecutor?

A. He supported the controversial California law.

B. He had no interest in putting the innocent in jail.

C. He intended to try a fifteen-year old suspect.

D. He wanted to try suspect as young as fourteen.

30. Which of the following is not true according to the text?

A. Pfingst's move didn't have a great coverage.

B. Pfingst's move greatly encouraged the jailed prisoners.

C. Pfingst's move didn't work well.

D. Pfingst's move had both the positive and negative effect.

44

Model Test 7

Directions: *In this part*, *you will have 15 minutes to go over the passage quickly and answer the questions on* **Answer Sheet 1**.

For questions 1 ~ 7, mark

Y (*for YES*)   *if the statement agrees with the information given in the passage;*

N (*for NO*)   *if the statement contradicts the information given in the passage;*

NG (*for NOT GIVEN*)   *if the information is not given in the passage.*

For questions 8 ~ 10, complete the sentences with the information given in the passage.

Are Americans too lazy

U.S. workers can't compete globally unless they work harder, writes Fortune's Geoff Colvin.

(*Fortune* Magazine) — We Americans pride ourselves on being a hard-working bunch, so here's a thought to spoil your Labor Day rest: By global standards, we're lazy. We've been getting lazier. And the days of the American dolce vita may be numbered.

The surprising report of our relative sloth arrives in new research from the UN's International Labor Organization, which looks at working hours around the world. When it comes to what we might call hard work, meaning the proportion of workers who put in more than 48 hours a week, America is near the bottom of the heap. About 18% of our employed people work that much.

That's a higher proportion than in a few other developed countries like Norway, the Netherlands, and even Japan. But it's actually lower than in Switzerland and Britain, and way lower than in developing countries like Mexico and Thailand. It's drastically lower than in what may be the world's two hardest-working countries, South Korea and Peru, where the proportions are about 50%.

Is America falling apart?

It's bad enough to be told we're slackers in the world economy. What many Americans really won't want to believe is separate research showing that we're working much less than we used to.

45

I know, I know — you're working harder than ever, and so is your spouse. But we're not talking about you; we're talking about the whole country, on average. And I'm afraid the findings are dramatic.

We have increased our leisure time enormously over the past 40 years — so much so that it "corresponds roughly to an additional five to ten weeks of vacation a year," says a study by Mark Aguiar of the Boston Fed and Erik Hurst of the University of Chicago business school, who conducted the study.

People with jobs are working fewer hours. Compounding the effect, fewer of us work at all, with growing numbers of people spending more time in retirement.

Of course, there's more to work than what we do on the job; there's also the work we do at home, and that too has fallen drastically. (It has fallen on average; men are actually doing a bit more work at home than they used to, but women are doing much less.)

What do you think?

Put it all together, and the researchers figure we're getting about 117 hours of leisure per week (including sleep), vs. 110 hours in 1965. That's more than 360 additional idle hours per year. We are a couch-potato nation.

You may wonder why I seem to be putting negative spin on these findings. Why should our massively expanded leisure be cause for anything but celebration?

After all, we're a much richer country than we were in 1965, and we're enjoying our wealth, just as economic theory would predict. Sweating less and having more is the whole idea.

The problem isn't what has happened, unless you figure we've just explained the obesity epidemic, but rather what might happen next. Every day more of us work in a global labor market, competing for jobs with people around the world. One thing markets do really well is fix disequilibrium; when anything tradable sells for different prices in different places, those differences soon disappear.

Americans and others in developed economies are selling the world's most expensive labor. In a global market, some of those prices — our pay — will have to stop rising and maybe even come down, while pay in China, India, and elsewhere goes up.

Economists see it happening already, attributing some of the surprising flatness in Americans' real total compensation of the past few years to the presence of millions of global workers competing for jobs.

A Cerberus deal goes bad ... and workers pay the price

That's one way that markets equilibrate. Another way may affect how hard we work. It's obvious that if real total pay is going nowhere, we may have to work harder just to improve our living standard.

46

More important, in the growing number of jobs not paid by the hour, people who work harder may just produce better results. General Electric chief Jeff Immelt put it bluntly while recalling a trip to Beijing last year, when he got a big order from the Transport Ministry: "The whole ministry was working all day on a Sunday. I believe in quality of life, work-life balance, all that stuff. But that's the competition. So unless we're willing to compete ..."

He has identified the issue. Competing in a global labor market may require us to put in more hours just to stay in the game. As Immelt asks, "Are we willing to compete for the future?"

Try to enjoy your Labor Day rest. You'll need it.

1. According to global standards, American are lazy.
2. In America, workers who work more than 48 hours a week are about 50%.
3. American haven't increased their leisure time in the past 40 years.
4. American women are doing less work at home than they used to.
5. The pay in China and India goes up in recent year.
6. American don't like to work extra hour without pay.
7. Competing in a global labor market may require people to put in more hours.
8. One thing markets do really well is fix disequilibrium; when anything tradable sells for different prices in different places, _____ .
9. It's obvious that if real total pay is going nowhere, _____ .
10. General Electric chief Jeff Immelt put it bluntly while recalling a trip to Beijing last year,
_____ .

Reading Comprehension (Reading in Depth) (25 minutes)
Section A
Directions: *In this section, there is a passage with ten blanks. You are required to select one word for each blank from a list of choices given in a word bank following the passage. Read the passage through carefully before making your choices. Each choice in bank is identified by a letter. Please mark the corresponding letter for each item on **Answer Sheet 2** with a single line through the center. **You may not use any of the words in the bank more than once**.*
Questions 11 to 20 are based on the following passage.

Technology is a two-edged sword. Rarely is this as clear as it is in the realm of health care. Technology allows doctors to test their patients for genetic defects—and then to turn around and spread the results __11__ the world via the Internet. For someone in need of treatment, that's good news. But for someone in search of a job or an insurance policy, the tidings can be all bad.

Last week President Bill Clinton proposed a corollary to the patients' bill of rights now before Congress: a right to medical ___12___ . Beginning in 2002, under rules set to become law in February, patients would be able to stipulate the conditions under which their personal medical data could be ___13___ . They would be able to examine their records and make corrections. They could learn who else had seen the ___14___ . Improper use of records by a caregiver or insurer could result in both civil and criminal penalties. The plan was, said Clinton, "an ___15___ __ step toward putting Americans back in control of their own medical records."

While the administration billed the rules as an ___16___ to strike a balance between the needs of consumers and those of the health-care industry, neither doctors nor insurance companies were happy. The doctors said the rules could actually erode privacy, pointing to a provision allowing managed-care plans to use personal information without ___17___ if the purpose was "health-care operations." That, physicians said, was a loophole through which HMOs and other insurers could pry into the doctor-patient relationship, in the name of assessing the quality of care. Meanwhile, the insurers ___18___ that the rules would make them vulnerable to lawsuits. They were especially disturbed by a provision holding them liable for privacy breaches by "business partners" such as lawyers and accountants. Both groups agreed that privacy protections would drive up the cost of health care by at least an additional $3.8 billion, and maybe much more, over the next five years. They also complained about the increased level of federal ___19___ required by the new rules' enforcement provisions.

One aim of the rules is to reassure patients about ___20___ , thereby encouraging them to be open with their doctors. Today various cancers and sexually transmitted diseases can go untreated because patients are afraid of embarrassment or of losing insurance coverage. The fear is real: Clinton aides noted that a January poll by Princeton Survey Research Associates found that one in six U.S. adults had at some time done something unusual to conceal medical information, such as paying cash for services.

A. attempt	I. unprecedented
B. disturbed	J. consent
C. protested	K. privacy
D. throughout	L. proposed
E. treatment	M. scrutiny
F. confidentiality	N. information
G. divulged	O. industry
H. of	

Section B

Directions: *There are 2 passages in this section. Each passage is followed by some questions or unfinished statements. For each of them are four choices marked A, B, C and D. You should*

48

decide on the best choice and mark the corresponding letter on **Answer Sheet 2** with a single line through the centre.

Passage One

Questions 21 to 25 are based on the following passage.

Five days before the opening move of Kasparov vs. the World, the chess champion sat in a fashionable Manhattan restaurant fighting off symptoms of a nasty head cold. Hunched over a cup of hot lemon juice and pinching his throat in pain, Garry Kasparov didn't look quite ready to rumble with the rest of the human race. Was this the world team's last, best hope at victory? Don't count on it. "There will," Kasparov says firmly, "be no mistakes in this game."

You'd better believe it. The tournament, which kicks off this Monday, pits the greatest living chess player in a single match against all comers on the Internet. Anybody who logs on (at www.zone.com) can vote on a variety of moves suggested by a panel of young grand masters. The most popular move is made; 24 hrs. later, Kasparov responds. And a few sniffles aren't likely to prevent the mighty Russian from beating amateur pawn pushers like you or me into a bloody pulp. "I don't expect us to win or anything," says Irina Krush, the 15-year-old U.S. women's chess champ and world-team coach, "but it'll be a fun game."

And a closely watched one too. Quite apart from being a timely test of war by committee (take note, NATO), it's Kasparov's first public confrontation with computer technology since his match with IBM's Deep Blue in 1997. Those games, billed as a historic confrontation between man and machine, ended with man's humiliating defeat (and petulant calls by Kasparov for IBM to hand over Deep Blue's printouts; two years later, they still refuse).

This time, however, man and machine will work in harmony—on both sides. Kasparov and many of his opponents will be consulting vast databases of past games and plotting computer-assisted strategies, a practice as common in chess now as using calculators to do long division. What's new here is the vast scale. In the long run, Kasparov vs. the World may tell us more about chess and human thought processes than Deep Blue ever could. "The result is irrelevant," says Kasparov, himself a part-time computer scientist and Internet addict. "It's a big experiment."

Indeed, you could say Kasparov is experimenting on us. The idea of playing a match in cyberspace was his, and the grand master has carefully controlled the setup from start to finish. He chose the game's host—Microsoft—for its software and marketing muscle. He insisted on up-and-coming chess prodigies to lead the world team—rather than more famous rivals like Anatoly Karpov or Nigel Short—so it wouldn't become a grudge match. And he set the 24-hr. gap between moves to ensure an antiseptic game, with none of the silly blunders you get in speed chess.

All well and good. But isn't there any way we lab rats can beat the chess scientist? Grand master Daniel King, who will do the commentary, thinks the sluggish time frame could actually work in our favor. Kasparov, he says, "thrives on pressure situations" and may play less aggressive chess at a leisurely pace. Let's hope so. Otherwise, we'll have to start rooting for the head cold.

21. What is Kasparov's attitude toward this match?

A. Annoyed.　　　　B. Proud.　　　　C. Confident.　　　　D. Concerned.

22. Which of the following is not the description of this match?

A. It is a confrontation between man and computer.

B. It is a match between one and the rest of the world.

C. The vast scale makes this match different from the former ones.

D. This match involves long match hours.

23. The expression "beating amateur pawn pushers like you or me into a bloody pulp" (Line 4, Paragraph 1) indicates that _____.

A. the amateurs have no intention to defeat Kasparov

B. the amateurs have great confidence in themselves

C. the amateurs can become mighty competitors

D. the common participants can be easily defeated

24. What is the author's attitude toward Kasparov?

A. Apprehensive.　　B. Respectful.　　　　C. Contemptible.　　D. Indifferent.

25. What is Kasparov's weak point in this game?

A. He has got a bad cold.　　　　　　　　B. He has too many rivals.

C. Less pressure makes him inactive.　　　D. The match hours are too short.

Passage Two

Questions 26 to 30 are based on the following passage.

It was a ruling that had consumers seething with anger and many a free trader crying foul. On November 20th the European Court of Justice decided that Tesco, a British supermarket chain, should not be allowed to import jeans made by America's Levi Strauss from outside the European Union and sell them at cut-rate prices without getting permission first from the jeans maker. Ironically, the ruling is based on an EU trademark directive that was designed to protect local, not American, manufacturers from price dumping. The idea is that any brand-owning firm should be allowed to position its goods and segment its markets as it sees fit: Levi's jeans, just like Gucci handbags, must be allowed to be expensive.

Levi Strauss persuaded the court that, by selling its jeans cheaply alongside soap powder and bananas, Tesco was destroying the image and so the value of its brands—which could only lead to less innovation and, in the long run, would reduce consumer choice. Consumer groups and Tesco say that Levi's case is specious. The supermarket argues that it was just arbitraging the price differential between Levi's jeans sold in America and Europe—a service performed a million times a day in financial markets, and one that has led to real benefits for consumers. Tesco has been selling some 15,000 pairs of Levi's jeans a week, for about half the price they command in specialist stores approved by Levi Strauss. Christine Cross, Tesco's head of global non-food sourcing, says the ruling risks "creating a Fortress Europe with a vengeance".

The debate will rage on, and has implications well beyond casual clothes (Levi Strauss was joined in its lawsuit by Zino Davidoff, a perfume maker). The question at its heart is not whether brands need to control how they are sold to protect their image, but whether it is the job of the courts to help them do this. Gucci, an Italian clothes label whose image was being destroyed by loose licensing and over-exposure in discount stores, saved itself not by resorting to the courts but by ending contracts with third-party suppliers, controlling its distribution better and opening its own stores. It is now hard to find cut-price Gucci anywhere.

Brand experts argue that Levi Strauss, which has been losing market share to hipper rivals such as Diesel, is no longer strong enough to command premium prices. Left to market forces, so-so brands such as Levi's might well fade away and be replaced by fresher labels. With the courts protecting its prices, Levi Strauss may hang on for longer. But no court can help to make it a great brand again.

26. Which of the following is not true according to Paragraph 1?

A. The ruling has protected Levi's from price dumping.

B. Only the Levi's maker can decide the prices of the jeans.

C. Consumers and free traders were very angry.

D. Levi's jeans should be sold at a high price .

27. Gucci's success shows that _____ .

A. it should be the court's duty to save its image

B. it has changed its fate with its own effort

C. opening its own stores is the key to success

D. gucci has successfully saved its own image

28. The word "specious"(Line 12, Para. 2) in the context probably means _____ .

A. responsible for oneself   B. having too many doubts

C. not as it seems to be   D. raising misunderstanding

29. According to the passage, the doomed fate of Levi's is caused by such factors except that

_____ .

A. the rivals are competitive   B. it fails to command premium prices

C. market forces have their own rules   D. the court fails to give some help

30. The author's attitude towards Levi's prospect seems to be _____ .

A. fair   B. subjective   C. puzzling   D. objective

Model Test 8

Part I   Reading Comprehension (Skimming and Scanning)   (15 minutes)

Directions: *In this part, you will have 15 minutes to go over the passage quickly and answer the questions on **Answer Sheet 1**.*

For questions 1 ~ 7, mark

Y (*for YES*)   *if the statement agrees with the information given in the passage;*

N (*for NO*)   *if the statement contradicts the information given in the passage;*

NG (*for NOT GIVEN*)   *if the information is not given in the passage.*

For questions 8 ~ 10, complete the sentences with the information given in the passage.

Living in the UK

We have always invested a great deal of effort and resources into the welfare and quality of life of our students. If problems of a non-academic nature crop up, there are helping hands that can give you guidance on financial and personal problems or health matters. You will usually have a course tutor or research supervisor who can be approached on a personal as well as academic basis.

International Office

This office was set up in 1995 to provide a focal point for existing and intending international students of the University. As well as tutoring many countries to show potential applicants what Brunel has to offer, we can give advice to international students on a whole range of matters, from financial difficulties and Home Office regulations to individual personal problems. At the start of each academic year, we organize an orientation program to help new international students adjust to life in the UK. Together with the Students' Union, the International Office also produces a handbook of pre-arrival information which is sent to all applicants from overseas in August. We also arrange a "meet and greet" scheme whereby new students arriving from overseas are met at Heathrow Airport and driven to their accommodation.

Students' Union

A students' union, or student council is a student organization present at many colleges and universities, dedicated to social and organizational activities of the student body.

The Students' Union, which represents the interests of all its members, provides many services, including two Information and Advice Centers. The purpose of the organization is to represent students' views within the university and sometimes on local and national issues. It is also responsible for providing a variety of services to students. Students can get involved in its management, through numerous and varied committees, councils and general meetings, or become one of its elected officers. In addition, the Union organizes over 16 ethic societies—Chinese and Hellenic, for example—which bring together students from different parts of the world, as well as more general social events with a multi-cultural emphasis.

Many students' unions are highly politicized bodies, and often serve as a training ground for aspiring politicians. Campaigning and debate is often very vigorous, with the youthful enthusiasm of the various partisans, a student media that is itself often partisan, inexperienced, and under no financial pressure to slant coverage to please a broad readership, and a general lack of serious consequences for decision all encouraging political gamesmanship. Some unions, however, are largely nonpolitical, and instead focus on providing on-campus recreation and retail facilities for students.

Student Recruiters

Students may exhibit their leadership through promotion of the University. The Office of Minority Affairs, the Visitor's Center, and many individual colleges utilize students in recruitment activities. Contact any of these offices for more information.

Christmas Party

There is a FREE BBQ in the park on the last day of school before the break for Christmas. Food and drink are provided and sports activities are arranged with the opportunity of winning prizes! There is also a college Christmas party that all students are invited to.

During the party, international Christmas carols are sung and then the celebrations begin with refreshments!

Information and Advice Centers

The Students' Union, with funding and cooperation from the University, runs two Information and Advice Centers, one at Uxbridge and one at Osterley. These aims to provide professional advice and information to all Brunel students about a wide range of issues, from immigration to the Council Tax. The staff of the Centers can help and advise overseas students in a variety of areas.

Campus Recreation

Campus Recreation utilizes students as intramural team managers, life guards, deck attendants, student office personnel, undergraduate assistants and sports officials.

Counselors

The University has an extensive network of trained counselors who are available to give advice to all students on personal or emotional problems.

Peer Education Leaders

There are several opportunities for peer education including: Peer Health Advocates through SHAC; Health Alcohol Education Program presenters through the Dean of Students Office; Academic Outreach Peer Presenters through the Learning Skills Program; Peer Mentors through the Office of Minority Affairs; and Peer Tutoring through SGA and the CATS program.

Student Activities Board (SAB)

SAB is a student group responsible for programming many of the special events and activities at UK. Students can develop leadership skills through involvement in one of the many SAB committees.

Medical Care

The Medical Centre houses a general medical practice on the Uxbridge Campus which is open throughout the year. Student residents on this campus or in the immediate surrounding area may therefore register with a doctor on campus. Students on the other three campuses must register with a doctor in their area. Free medical care under the UK National Health Service is normally available to all overseas students at Brunel provided that: a) they are registered with the University as an overseas student or are a dependent of one and , b) they are seeking treatment for a complaint which has developed since registration. It is essential to bring to the UK a certificate signed by your own doctor stating that your health is good.

Dental care is not provided by the University and students will need to register with a local NHS practice (non-NHS practices charge more for treatment).

You can also obtain further information before coming to the UK from the Department of Health, Alexander Fleming House, London SEI 6BY, or the Department of Social Security (overseas branch), Castle Buildings Stormont, Belfast, BT43HH, N Ireland.

Role of the British Council

The Council's headquarters, based in central London, organizes trips, courses and other activities for overseas visitors. It also publishes a book called "How to live in Britain".

1. The University began to enroll international students after 1995.
2. New international students take the orientation program free of charge.
3. A Chinese student in the UK must join the Student's Union.
4. Overseas students must register with a doctor on campus.
5. Cost for treatment of an illness developed before one comes to the UK is not covered by the university.
6. Cost for dental care is covered by the NHS.
7. The British Council organizes free trips for overseas students.
8. New students arriving from overseas are met at _____.

54

9. Information about immigration or council tax can be obtained from _____.

10. Students' emotional problems may be solved by _____.

Part II Reading Comprehension (Reading in Depth) (25 minutes)

Section A

Directions: *In this section, there is a passage with ten blanks. You are required to select one word for each blank from a list of choices given in a word bank following the passage. Read the passage through carefully before making your choices. Each choice in the bank is identified by a letter. Please mark the corresponding letter for each item on **Answer Sheet 2** with a single line through the centre. **You may not use any of the words in the bank more than once**.*

Questions 11 to 20 are based on the following passage.

One day a police officer managed to get some fresh mushrooms. He was so pleased with what he had bought that he offered to __11__ the mushrooms with his brother officers. When their breakfast arrived the next day, each officer found some mushrooms on his plate.

"Let the dog try a piece first," suggested one __12__ officer who was afraid that the mushrooms might be poisonous. The dog seemed to enjoy his mushrooms, and the officers then began to eat their meal saying that the mushrooms had a very strange but quite pleasant __13__.

An hour later, however, they were all astonished when the gardener rushed in and said __14__ the dog was dead. Immediately the officers jumped to their cars and rushed to the nearest __15__. Pumps were used and the officers had a very hard time getting rid of the mushrooms that remained in their __16__. When they returned to the police station, they sat down and started to __17__ the mushroom poisoning. Each man explained the pains that he had felt and they agreed that these had grown worse on their way to the hospital. The gardener was called to tell the way in which the poor dog had died. "Did it __18__ much before death?" asked one of the officers, feeling very pleased that he had escaped a __19__ death himself." "No," the gardener looked rather __20__. "It was killed the moment a car hit it."

A. frightened	I. strange
B. seriously	J. share
C. refuse	K. curiously
D. hospital	L. taste
E. discuss	M. comfortable
F. careful	N. painful
G. surprised	O. suffer
H. stomachs	

Section B

Directions: *There are 2 passages in this section. Each passage is followed by some questions or unfinished statements. For each of them there are four choices marked A, B, C and D. You should decide on the best choice and mark the corresponding letter on **Answer Sheet 2** with a single line through the centre.*

Passage One

Questions 21 to 25 are based on the following passage.

London's taxi drivers scare politicians stiff. The thought of the city's 24,000 cabbies bad-mouthing them to several dozen passengers a day has discouraged successive governments from trying to reform the archaic regulations that protect licensed taxis. So when, 18 months ago, Ken Livingstone took on the responsibility for regulating cabbies and promised to reform the trade, ministers were relieved and the voters applauded.

There are not so many cheers now. The mayor decided to smooth the path of change by giving cabbies the largest fare increase they have ever had, through a surcharge that kicks in at 8 p.m.. London's cabs are now among the most expensive in the world. Night-time taxi fares have risen by as much as 60%, depending on the length of the journey. Even in the daytime, a journey from Heathrow airport to the center of the city costs upwards of £40.

Bill Oddy, general secretary of the London Taxi Drivers' Association (LTDA), strongly defends the increases, and says he is "proud" of London's high ranking, pointing out that more cabs are available for hire than ever before. But even many cab drivers believe that fares have risen too far, too fast. Rodney Lewis, managing editor of the trade paper, Taxi Globe, says that the price rises were "appallingly handled".

But Mr. Oddy says prices had to go up if the supply of drivers was to rise. But the shortage of drivers is a consequence of the absurdly tight regulation of London cabs, which imposes other costs on the trade and therefore on passengers. A new cab, for instance, costs £26,000—twice as much as a standard saloon—partly because it has to be able to perform a U-turn in less than 7.62 m. Some regulations, dating back to Victorian times, are aimed at horse-drawn carriages.

21. The London government has failed to launch reform on its taxis because _____.

A. old regulations still protect licensed taxis

B. it can not afford to offend those bad-mouthing drivers

C. London's taxi drivers are closely linked to influential politicians

D. dozens of drivers have discouraged the government from carrying out such reform

22. It can be inferred from the first paragraph that _____.

A. people have longed for ages for the government to regulate this trade

B. most London taxi drivers are scared of powerful politicians

56

C. passengers have urged the government to take on more responsibilities

D. London taxi drivers will go on strike as soon as reform starts

23. We can learn from the passage that the huge fare increase _____.

A. will affect the economy of Great Britain profoundly

B. is allowed to pave the way for the reform

C. will crush night-time taxi service thoroughly

D. will scare the majority of European passengers off

24. The majority of people think of the new taxi fare as _____.

A. too low   B. reasonable   C. too high   D. offensive

25. Who benefits least from the reform according to the passage?

A. Taxi drivers.   B. The government.

C. The London Taxi Drivers' Association.   D. Passengers.

Passage Two

Questions 26 to 30 are based on the following passage.

Choosing the right job is probably one of the most important decisions we have to make in life, and it is frequently one of the hardest decisions we have to make. One important question that you might ask yourself is: "How do I get a good job?" People find jobs in an infinite number of ways.

There are people who can answer an insignificant advertisement in the local paper and land the best job in the world; others write to all sorts of places all over the country, and never seem to get a reply at all. Still others believe that the in-person, door-to-door approach is by far the best way to get a job; and then there are those who, through no active decision of their own, just seem to be in the right place at the right time. Take the young man who wanted to be a sailor. He used to spend a lot of his free time down by the sea watching the tall ships, but never thinking that he might one day sail one of them. His father was a farmer, and being a sailor could never be anything for the boy but an idle dream. One day, on his usual wandering, he heard the captain of the ship complaining that he could not sail because one member of his crew was sick. Without stopping to think, the lad offered to take his place. He spent the rest of his life happily sailing the ships he had always loved.

This story also illustrates the importance of seizing an opportunity when it presents itself. If the lad had gone home to ponder his decision for a week, he may have missed his chance. It is one thing to be offered an opportunity; it is another thing to take it and use it well.

Sometimes we hear stories about people who break all the rules and still seem to land the *plum jobs*(美差). When you go for a job interview or fill out an application, you are expected to say nice things about the company to which you are applying. But there was one person who landed an excellent job by telling the interviewer all the company's faults. And within a year this person had become general manager of the company.

26. According to the author, one can find a job _____.

A. in numerous ways   B. as long as one wants to

C. with the help of other people   D. only when one has a good education

27. It can be inferred from the passage that _____.

A. it's almost impossible to find a good job by answer advertisement in newspapers

B. it is very hard for some people to obtain a satisfactory job

C. no one believes that the in-person, door-to-door approach is the best way to get a job

D. only those lucky people can find a good job

28. Which of the following statements is NOT true?

A. It is very important to seize an opportunity when it presents itself.

B. The young man in the story has never wanted to become a sailor.

C. Some people can get a good job without any effort.

D. Not everybody can take and use an opportunity well when it presents itself.

29. Which of the following best described the style of this article?

A. Analytic and logically precise.   B. Easy-going mind light.

C. Seriously business like.   D. Funny, full of humor.

30. From the last paragraph of this passage we can learn that _____.

A. people can get a good job only if they say nice things about the company to which they are applying

B. sometimes it can be wise to pick out some of your potential employer's faults in his/her operation of the company

C. the man's boss likes all the employees who are critical of him

D. only when you can find out the boss's faults can you land an excellent job

58

Part Ⅱ 模拟阅读试题
答案及解析

Model Test 1

Part I Reading Comprehension (Skimming and Scanning)

1. [答案]Y

[解析]该句句意为：巨大的河流改道水利工程导致咸海水量减少。解题依据为第二段倒数第二句话"As a result, the sea has shrunk to half its original size...",意思是"结果,咸海缩减至原来的一半……",与原文之意吻合。

2. [答案]N

[解析]该句句意为：巨坝和灌溉工程的建设好处多于坏处。解题依据为本文第三段第二句话"But many countries continue to build massive dams and irrigation systems, even though such projects can create more problems than they fix",意思为"虽然产生更多问题,但许多国家仍继续建巨坝和灌溉工程"。由此可知,坏处多于好处,所以该题与原文之意不符。

3. [答案]Y

[解析]该句句意为：缺水的主要原因是人口增长和水污染。解题依据可定位到本文第四段第一句话"Growing populations will worsen problems with water..."及第十一段第一句话"But almost everyone contributes to water pollution",两者都是水资源缺乏的原因,与原文之意相符。

4. [答案]Y

[解析]该句句意为：美国人面临的有关水的问题为地下水的减少和污染。解题依据为第七段第二句话和第八段第三句话,这两句话加在一起即为美国人所面临的水资源方面的问题,与原文之意相符。

5. [答案]N

[解析]该句句意为：根据这篇文章,所有的水污染都来自于家庭废弃物。解题依据为第十一段最后一句话"...70 percent of the pollutants could be traced to household waste",意思为"70%的污染物源于家庭废弃物"。据此,本题之意与原文之意不合。

6. [答案]N

[解析]该句句意为：美国人将不会面临缺水问题。解题依据为文章第七段第二句话"But Americans could face serious water shortages, too, especially in areas that rely on groundwater",显然本题之意与原文之意不符。

7. [答案]NG

[解析]该句句意为：水利专家 Gleick 提供了与水相关的最佳解决方案。根据本文第十三段第一句话所述,专家 Gleick 并未提供任何最佳解决方案。

8.[答案]one third

[解析]解题依据为第四段最后一句话。

9.[答案]glaciers and ice caps

[解析]解题依据为第五段第二句话。

10.[答案]water pollution

[解析]解题依据为第十段第二句话。

Part Ⅱ Reading Comprehension(Reading in Depth)

Section A

11.[答案]D

[解析]从空格后的谓语动词"have"可知该处应填入复数名词,因此,只能在 D 和 M 中选择;由于和"drop 10 percentage points"搭配,此处应填入"比例"一词,所以 D 为正确选项。

12.[答案]F

[解析]本题难度很大,只能根据完成时态,先排除 C 和 O 两项,然后结合对上下文的理解,作者悲叹年轻人读的书太少,"如果你只读了青少年杂志上的一篇小故事,那也被计算在内"。因此正确的选项是 F。

13.[答案]O

[解析]该题较为简单,依据本文的一般现在时态、单数主语和后面的介词 to 可以推断出正确答案,"attribute...to"意为"把……归因于……"。

14.[答案]L

[解析]根据文章的意思、时态和单复数的基本知识可知选 L。

15.[答案]K

[解析]因为在 by 之后,这里只能采用动名词的形式。所给选项 3 个动名词中意思符合的一项即 K(force somebody to do)。

16.[答案]N

[解析]本句结构工整,"from _____ vocabulary to stretching imagination",显然应填入一个动名词,根据文章的意思,应该填入 N,意为"从构建词汇量到拓展思维能力"。

17.[答案]J

[解析]release...from 是固定搭配。

18.[答案]C

[解析]根据上下文含义,可知"17 岁从不或者很少读书的孩子数量上升",本题与下一题题句式相同,但意思相反,因此从下文的 drop 一词也可推断出本题的正确选项。

19.[答案]E

[解析]结合上下文,该处应填入一个意为"比例"的名词,即 E 项 percentage。此处

考生应该注意"percentage"(比例)与"percent"(具体的百分比)的区别。选项 percentage 与上句的 number 对应。

20. [答案]B

[解析]此处根据助动词 have 和形容词 constant,可知该处应该填入一个系动词的过去分词,意为"保持不变",只能填入 remained。

Section B

Passage One

21. [答案]B

[解析]细节理解题。该题有一定难度。根据题干,解答该题应定位在第一段。第一段第二行说"它有时放在'situations vacant'(招聘栏目)",其中招聘加了引号,再加上随后的让步从句明确否定了给人提供工作,所以 A 项应排除。第三行说"它有时放在'situations wanted'(求职栏目)",随后的让步从句也明确否定了 D 项。而选择正确答案应根据最后一句话"What it does is to offer help in applying for a job"。C 项意思为"把现有的工作分成各种类型",文章没有提及,也应排除。

22. [答案]C

[解析]细节理解题。解答该题只需正确理解第二段第二行"The growth and apparent success of such a specialized service is, of course, a reflection on the current high levels of unemployment",意为"这种特别服务的出现和成功反映了当今的高失业率"。这正是 C 项的内容。该题属倒着考题型。

23. [答案]D

[解析]细节理解题。最关键的提示句应该是第三段第三句"The letter was really just for openers, it was explained, everything else could and should be saved for the interview"。言外之意,在信中不必写得太详细,应该在得到面试机会后再透露更多细节。D 项为正确选项。

24. [答案]A

[解析]细节理解题。文章第四段第一行中的"as you moved up the ladder"与题干中的"as one went on to apply for more important jobs"对应。因此,随后的内容"something slightly more sophisticated was called for. The advice then was to put something in the letter which would distinguish you from the rest"即为正确答案。B 项意为"有关申请人个性的隐含信息";C 项意为"申请人申请工作时相对于其他人的优势"。这两项均不正确。D 项意为"用主动积极的方法偶尔玩点花招",只是引人关注的其中一种方法,不如 A 项具有概括性。

25. [答案]B

[解析]单句理解题。本题问个人履历为什么重要。学生只要正确理解最后一段,就可做出正确选择,最后一句实际上是强调句型:"... it is increasing number of applicants with university education at all points in the process of engaging staff that has led to the greater importance of the curriculum vitae",明确讲明是越来越多的具有大学教育背景的求职者使得个人履历更显重要。"it is"后的内容也即 B 项的内容,所以 B 项正确。A、C、D 项文中都没有涉及,均应排除。

Passage Two

26.[答案]A

[解析]细节理解题。本题问规定最高租金可能会导致什么结果。文章第一段明确指出,"landlords"(房东)收取租户的租金有了最高限额,他们的利润会受到影响,也可能导致他们投资其他行业,鉴于此,C、D 两项都是错误的。B 项"使租房为家的人担忧"文中没有涉及,也不对。依据第一段最后一句话"the end result of rent control is a shortage of apartments in the city",可知 A 项为正确选项。

27.[答案]C

[解析]细节理解题。依据第一段第四句"However, the critics say that after a long time, rent control may have negative effects",可断定 C 项正确。A、B、D 项都含绝对意味,不符合文中意思。

28.[答案]A

[解析]细节理解题。解答该题只要准确理解第二段的含义,尤其从第三行开始"However, if the minimum is high, ... Thus, critics claim, an increase in the minimum wage may cause unemployment"。

29.[答案]B

[解析]主旨题。本文从 rent control 和最低工资控制两方面讨论了政府控制可能造成的后果。进一步说,许多政府行为可能保护某些利益,但从长远看,也会带来许多问题。B 项正确。A 项意为"(文章叙述了)供需关系";C 项意为"(文章叙述了)政府控制的必要性";D 项意为"(文章叙述了)摆脱政府控制的紧迫性"。文章并没有深入谈及这三项内容,显然不能成为文章主旨。

30.[答案]D

[解析]细节判断题。依据第四段第二行"The predictions may be correct only if 'other things are equal'"可知 A 项是对的。从第二段可得知规定最低工资会使得雇主雇用更少的工人,会考虑用机器替代工人,也就会导致更多的人失业,所以 B 项是可以成立的说法。C 项的内容实际上是 A 项的另一种说法,也可成立。依据第四段内容,可得知 D 项不正确。经济理论应该有相当的参考价值,只是还需考虑方方面面的因素。

Model Test 2

Part I Reading Comprehension (Skimming and Scanning)

1. [答案]N

[解析]本题问"在附近开诊所的家庭医生和送早报的年轻人都不是创业者"这一说法是否正确。文章第一段第二句"The truth is that we often fail to recognize entrepreneurs all around us..."指出:事实是,我们常常认不出我们周围的创业者,如拐角杂货店的老板、在附近开诊所的家庭医生、送早报的年轻人。

2. [答案]Y

[解析]本题问"创办一个成功的新企业的要素是机会、创业者和资源"这一说法是否正确。文章第二段第一句明确指出"there are three crucial components for a successful new venture: the opportunity, the entrepreneur, and the resources needed to start the company and make it grow"。

3. [答案]N

[解析]本题问"创办并发展公司所需的资源包括资金、过程和技术"这一说法是否正确。文章第二段倒数第二句明确指出"Resources include money, people and skill"。

4. [答案]Y

[解析]本题问"比尔盖茨和报纸投递员的区别在于他们期望获得的商业成功程度不同"这一说法是否正确。文中第三段第一句明确指出"One factor which distinguishes Bill Gates from the morning paper deliverer is the level of business success each desires to achieve"。

5. [答案]N

[解析]本题问"定义成功有助于有效地评价公司潜能"这一说法是否正确。文章"Defining Success through Personal Evaluation"小节最后一段第二句指出"How we define success significantly influences our selection of a business to start"。

6. [答案]NG

[解析]本题问"出国深造也有助于实现个人的未来定位"这一说法是否正确。文章"Visioning and Goal Setting for Business Success"小节阐述如何给自己定位并为自己确定目标,没有提到这一点。

7. [答案]Y

[解析]本题问"确定目标是实现你的生活定位的行动计划"这一说法是否正确。文章"Visioning and Goal Setting for Business Success"小节第三段中明确指出这一点。

8. [答案]discard the idea

[解析]"Defining Success through Personal Evaluation"小节倒数第三句指出："If we think a business opportunity has the potential to raise us to our desired level of success, we give it further consideration. If not, we usually discard the idea."

9. [答案]guidance and direction

[解析]"Visioning and Goal Setting for Business Success"小节第二段第二句指出："The vision of ourselves is the foundation that will give us guidance and direction in the conduct of our lives and business."

10. [答案]tools

[解析]文章最后一句指出："Visioning and goal-setting are tools you can use to develop a clear picture of who you are, where you are going and what you need to do to get there."

Part II Reading Comprehension (Reading in Depth)

Section A

11. [答案]J

[解析]固定搭配,live through 意为"度过、经历过"。句意为:如果你曾经在芝加哥度过冬天,那么全球变暖听上去一点也不坏。

12. [答案]E

[解析]increase 意为"增加"。句意为:但是全球变暖的影响之一就是暴风雨增加。

13. [答案]A

[解析]severe 意为"剧烈的"。句意为:研究报道近年来强风暴增加了20%。

14. [答案]M

[解析]consequence 意为"结果"。句意为:全球变暖的另一个结果是……

15. [答案]G

[解析]melt 意为"融化"。句意为:全球变暖的另一个结果是冰河逐渐融化。

16. [答案]B

[解析]float 意为"漂浮"。句意为:大西洋大块的冰冠断裂漂走。

17. [答案]H

[解析]summit 意为"顶点"。句意为:南美安第斯山脉的冰峰正在消失。

18. [答案]L

[解析]rely 意为"依靠"。句意为:这对那些依靠融化的雪水灌溉庄稼的农民来说境况堪忧。

19. [答案]D

[解析]raise 意为"提高"。句意为:已经表明,融化的雪水将提升海平面。

20. [答案]O

[解析]above 意为"在……上方"。句意为:人类使用的许多土地仅位于海平面以上一英尺或更少。

Section B

Passage One

21. [答案]D

[解析]文章第四段提到,研究人员发现学习能力缺陷者的脑细胞颜色为灰色,而正常人为白色,并且神经细胞的排列方式不同,因此 D 为正确答案。

22. [答案]A

[解析]只有选项 A 的内容未提及。

23. [答案]C

[解析]只有选项 C 的陈述有误。学习能力缺陷是一个常见问题,其影响范围为儿童的 10%,而不是全部人口的 10%。

24. [答案]B

[解析]全文的最后一句话提供了答案。Duffy 医生说他的研究表明学习能力缺陷涉及大脑大面积损伤而不仅限于左半脑。

25. [答案]A

[解析]全文并没有就影响大脑发育和构成的因素达成一致的看法,仍需进一步研究,因此选项 A 为正确答案。

Passage Two

26. [答案]B

[解析]文章第一段明确指出"The change was based on the findings of many market studies. These studies had shown that the general response to the new product was good",因此选项 B 为正确答案。

27. [答案]D

[解析]文章第二段第一句指出,新可乐被拒绝的最重要原因是饮用者与老配方之间存在情感联系,因此选项 D 为正确答案。

28. [答案]A

[解析]文章第二段第三句指出,公司改变的不仅是可乐的配方,还有它所代表的传统价值和回忆。因此选项 A 为正确答案。

29. [答案]C

[解析]文章第三段对可口可乐公司所有的调查作了分析,尽管公司作了大量调查,但却没有考虑因为老式传统可乐的消失而造成的个人情感反应。因此选项 C 为正确答案。

30. [答案]C

[解析]文章最后一句点明了答案,因此选 C。

Model Test 3

Part I　Reading Comprehension（Skimming and Scanning）

1.［答案］Y

［解析］本题问"当人们说'他（或她）从来不听'时,是指他（或她）应该为过失负责任"这一说法是否正确。根据文章第一段判断,该陈述是正确的。

2.［答案］Y

［解析］本题问"倾听不同于听见,是因为倾听需要获得更多的额外信息"这一说法是否正确。根据文章第三段判断该陈述是正确的。

3.［答案］Y

［解析］本题问"要做一名好的倾听者,你的眼睛和耳朵必须紧密结合"这一说法是否正确。文章第六段最后一句指出："Being a good listener involves being a good watcher: eyes and ears must go hand in hand."

4.［答案］NG

［解析］本题问"如果某人直视说话者,眼神没有焦距,通常说明他感到很无趣"这一说法是否正确。文中第七段对部分身体语言作了说明,该陈述没有提及。

5.［答案］Y

［解析］本题问"和别人交谈时不要不耐烦地打断别人或草草做出结论"这一说法是否正确。文章后半部分引述了美国心理学家 Robert C. Beck 提出的自我改进规则"Be patient"中指出："...don't interrupt impatiently or jump to conclusions."

6.［答案］N

［解析］本题问"和聪明人交谈时,多数人会变得更健谈"这一说法是否正确。文章后半部分引述了美国心理学家 Robert C. Beck 提出的自我改进规则"Don't be too clever"中指出："faced with a know-all, many people become silent, ..."

7.［答案］Y

［解析］本题问"谈话中让对方解释你没有完全理解的地方或词语"这一说法是否正确。文章后半部分引述了美国心理学家 Robert C. Beck 提出的自我改进规则"Ask for explanations"中指出："get people to explain points or words you have not fully understood"。

8.［答案］faultless

［解析］第一段最后一句指出:我们都大声地责备别人,假装我们自己是无可指责的。

9.［答案］the speakers' body language

[解析]第六段第一句指出："One of the key ways to improve your listening ability is by learning to keep a watchful eye on the speakers' body language."

10.[答案]grasped the correct messages

[解析]文章最后一段指出："It ensures you have listened accurately and grasped the correct messages."

Part II　Reading Comprehension (Reading in Depth)

Section A

11.[答案]K

[解析]unfortunately 意为"不幸地"。本句与上一句为转折关系,句意为:不幸的是,疾病或事故有可能毫无预警地发生。

12.[答案]B

[解析]固定搭配,capable of 意为"能够……"。句意为:如果家里有人能够按照医生的指导照顾病人,病人可以在家里照料。

13.[答案]G

[解析]treatment 意为"治疗"。句意为:有时可以安排护士上门进行每天一次或多次治疗。

14.[答案]A

[解析]interval 意为"时间间隔"。句意为:护士上门护理的间歇由家里负责照顾病人的人进行护理。

15.[答案]N

[解析]distinct 意为"不同的",be distinct from 意为"不同于……"。句意为:……完全不同于家庭护理。

16.[答案]O

[解析]affect 意为"影响"。句意为:当疾病降临时,整个家庭都受到影响。

17.[答案]D

[解析]disturb 意为"打扰、扰乱"。句意为:……但是家庭日常作息不必完全被扰乱。

18.[答案]J

[解析]strain 意为"紧张"。句意为:可重新安排家庭职责来节省时间和经历,从而减轻家人的紧张。

19.[答案]L

[解析]assume 意为"承担、担任"。句意为:护理通常由一个人负责。

20.[答案]E

[解析]moreover 意为"此外、而且"。本句与上一句为递进关系。

Section B

Passage One

21. [答案]D

[解析]细节判断题。根据第一段第三句和第四句:他们也想定高价以获取高额收益,但行业内的竞争往往不允许他们这样做。一般地说,如果竞争对手不抬高价格,商家不会提高自己产品的价格。因此选 D。

22. [答案]D

[解析]词义题,这里考术语"the most productive input-mix"的概念。这个术语出现在第二段结尾,其定义是该句中"is called"前面的部分"the combination of inputs that permits a firm to produce its goods or services at the lowest possible cost without reducing quality"。意为"允许一家公司在最大限度地降低成本而又不降低品质的情况下生产产品或提供服务的投入组合"。这一组合包括两方面内容,即降低成本并保持质量,因此选 D。

23. [答案]C

[解析]细节题。本题考查对第三段的理解。根据第二句"The resources an industry needs and the customers it serves are rarely close to each other"可直接判断,因此选 C。

24. [答案]A

[解析]细节题。本题关键词"the soft drink industry and the paper making industry"在第四段,两个行业一个是 weight-gaining,一个是 weight-losing,因此选 A。

25. [答案]B

[解析]主旨题。本文说明企业如何降低生产成本,以增加竞争力,因此选 B。

Passage Two

26. [答案]C

[解析]词义题。结合上下文,第一段前面部分都是关于美貌的好处,最后一句用了转折连词 but,因此后面的意思与前面内容相反,即美貌的不利之处,而且后文也主要谈美貌的种种不利之处,因此选项 C 为正确答案。

27. [答案]A

[解析]以关键词"traditionally female jobs"以及第六段第三句为依据。该句指出:因此,有吸引力的女人在传统的女性职业中占有优势。因此选项 A 为正确答案。

28. [答案]D

[解析]文章最后两段谈论了有吸引力在政治方面的影响,最后一段引用了 Bowman 的实验结果:相貌出众的男候选人最终击败了相貌平庸的男候选人,而被认为最漂亮的女候选人却总是获得最低的支持率。因此选项 D 为正确答案。

29. [答案]B

[解析]根据常识,一个人的相貌和工作态度、能力等没有固定的、必然的联系,而文章讨论的内容是,人们认为这两点有联系,所以人们对于美貌的看法是"有偏见

的",因此选项 B 为正确答案。

30. [答案]A

[解析]综观全文,本文主要讨论美貌(或有吸引力)对某些职业的不利影响,因此选项 A 为正确答案。

Model Test 4

Part I Reading Comprehension(Skimming and Scanning)

1. [答案]Y

[解析]本题问"在大学的四年期间共有 100 次期中及期末考试"这一说法是否正确。文章第四段第二句指出:"college mid-term and final examinations over a four-year period account for another 100",意为"大学的期中及期末考试加在一起共有 100 次"。这与题干相符,因此本题正确。

2. [答案]Y

[解析]本题问"由政府、企业和行业组织的各种考试的数量要远远大于学校组织的考试"这一说法是否正确。文章第六段明确指出:"The total number administered by business, government, industry and clinics, however, is *astronomical*(庞大无法估计的), dwarfing the total number of school tests.""dwarfing"意为 "多于;优于……",此句与题干相符,因此本题正确。

3. [答案]N

[解析]本题问"maximal performance 给人带来的焦虑要比 typical performance 给人带来的焦虑少"这一说法是否正确。文章第十八段第一句明确指出:"Typical performance tests do not promote as much anxiety as maximal-performance tests." 这与题干相反,因此本题错误。

4. [答案]N

[解析]本题问"如果你到考场较早,你应该独自一人待着并且要复习一下资料"这一说法是否正确。文章在介绍考试技巧部分的第二条中明确指出"If you must get there early, stand alone, away from the crowd",此句只说明了题干的一部分,并没有说明是否要复习的问题。因此本题错误。

5. [答案]N

[解析]本题问"如果对所猜的题没有把握,就选择最短的答案"这一说法是否正确。文章在介绍考试技巧部分的第四条第四句指出:"... if there is no correction for guessing, then pick the longest answer and proceed to the next test question." 这恰恰与题干相反,因此本题错误。

6. [答案]Y

[解析]本题问"如果对某题不确定,你应该做下一题,等想起来再回过来做这道题"这一说法是否正确。文章在介绍考试技巧部分的第十条中明确指出:"Skip items you are unsure of, items about material you've seen before but can't remember the answer

71

immediately. Chances are your brain will be searching for and *retrieving*（重新得到）the information while you are working on other items. When the answer comes to you, go back and mark it."这与题干相符,因此本题正确。

7.[答案]N

[解析]本题问"有证据表明,如果冷静,你在考试中就不会表现好"这一说法是否正确。文章在介绍考试技巧部分的第十三条中明确指出:"There is some evidence that if you are slightly cool you will do better on a test."这恰恰与题干相反,因此本题错误。

8.[答案]Maximal tests

[解析]文章第十三段第二句指出:"Maximal tests attempt to measure an individual's best possible performance accurately."

9.[答案]admissions test

[解析]文章第十六段第一句指出:"Another maximal-performance test is an admissions test（technically a form of aptitude testing）."

10.[答案]necessary

[解析]文章倒数第二段第一句指出:"Tests are necessary to determine levels of know ledge and to help make placement decisions."

Part II Reading Comprehension（Reading in Depth）

Section A

11.[答案]E

[解析]honor 意为"纪念"。句意为:……纪念希腊的神。

12.[答案]K

[解析]physical fitness 意为"身体的健康协调"。句意为:希腊重视年轻人身体的协调与力量。

13.[答案]C

[解析]contests 意为"比赛,竞技比赛"。

14.[答案]M

[解析]individual 意为"个别的"。句意为:……比赛将在某个特定城市举办。

15.[答案]J

[解析]participants 意为"参赛者"。句意为:参赛者每 4 年将在奥林匹亚山上竞技角逐。

16.[答案]B

[解析]此处需要副词,greatly 意为"大大地"。句意为:获胜者将受到大大的奖励……

17.[答案]N

[解析]Originally,此处需要首写字母大写。句意为:最初这些比赛是为了友谊的目的。

18.［答案］G

［解析］in progress 意为"继续",固定搭配。句意为:正在进行的战争……

19.［答案］D

［解析］attach importance to 意为"重视",固定搭配。句意为:希腊人如此重视这些比赛,以至于他们每 4 年就要举办一届名为"Olympiads"的运动会。

20.［答案］F

［解析］cycles 意为"循环"。句意为:希腊人如此重视这些比赛,以至于他们每 4 年就要举办一届名为"Olympiads"的运动会。

Section B

Passage One

21.［答案］D

［解析］本文开头简要介绍了 backpacking 这种活动的起源。但这不是文中主要讨论的内容。因为作者接下来重点阐述了 backpacking 作为一种现代娱乐活动深受很多人喜爱是因为它可以考验一个人的耐力和生存技巧,不受时间限制等等。可以看出,文中讨论的重点是 backpacking 作为一种现代娱乐活动为什么会深受许多人喜爱。D 选项与此意相同,说明了文章的中心议题,符合题意,是正确答案。

22.［答案］B

［解析］原文开头提到"Except for the Indians, the earliest backpackers in America were frontiersmen",除了印第安人,frontiersmen(未开发的边疆居民)是美国最早的 back-packers。这说明 Indians 才是美国最早的 backpackers。因此 B 选项是正确答案。

23.［答案］D

［解析］本文开头提到"…, the earliest backpackers…, who roamed the wilderness looking either for necessities such as food and water or for sources of wealth such as fur and gold…"最早的 backpackers…,游荡在原野里,寻找诸如水和食物这样的生存必需品或者像毛皮和黄金之类的财源。因此说早期的 backpackers 最需要、最感兴趣的是生活必需品。因为生存是第一需要,而他们生存的依靠就是在漫游中不断地寻找生存的基本需要。D 项与此意相符,是正确答案。A 项是实现"美国梦"的途径。文中说:"For them backpacking was a way of survival or a means of achieving what one day would be called the 'American Dream'."注意文中用的是过去将来时,也就是说早期的 backpackers 还没有"美国梦"这个概念,是他们以后的人创造发明的。因此,此说法与文意不符。B 项是生活中的娱乐。文中说:"For them backpacking was a way of survival",对于早期的 backpackers 来说,背着包袱漫游是他们生存的手段。因此不能说他们是为了寻找生活中的乐趣。另外,后文中也提到:"Today, however, many people enjoy backpacking as a recreational activity."这说明,把背着背包漫游当作一种娱乐活动是现代人的事情。C 项意为"从紧张的生活中得以解脱"。文中说这是早期 backpackers 的一种生存方式,也就是他们的生活活动,因此不能说

是他们从紧张生活中得以解脱。

24．[答案]A

[解析]它(backpacking)可以帮助人们与自然建立一种联系。文中说："Shouldering a pack and leaving behind the world of telephone, television, and traffic promise an exciting experience. Testing one's *stamina*（耐力）and skills are challenging a sense of one's place in the natural world can be rewarding."挎上背包,把由电话、电视和交通构成的世界抛在脑后,你将有一次激动人心的经历,作为回报,你将通过挑战人在自然世界的位置的概念来检验自身的耐力和技巧。这说明在这项活动中,人融入自然,属于自然世界的一部分,它在人和自然之间建立了一种直接的联系。这也是这项活动的好处所在。因此A项答案是正确的。B项意为"它是一种群体活动,可以治疗一个人的孤独感";C项意为"它不像其他活动一样富有挑战性";D项意为"它不要求人们决定自己的目标"。均非文中讨论的内容。

25．[答案]C

[解析]原文最后一句："Their outing will enable them to return in a short time to the age of technology with the courage and independence of Natty Bumppo, who did indeed belong to the age of the frontier."短暂的出游活动可以使他们回到Natty Bumppo(生活)的技术与勇气和自立相结合的时代,他实实在在是属于边疆时代的。C项意为"一个勇敢的人",符合文中的叙述,是正确的答案。A项意为"一个美国民族英雄";B项意为"海明威小说中的主人公";D项意为"一名印第安士兵"。文中均没提到。

Passage Two

26．[答案]B

[解析]从文中第一句可以找到答案："They are among the 250,000 people under the age of 25 who are out of work in the Netherlands, a group that accounts for 40 percent of the nation's unemployed." 250 000名低于25岁的青年失业者占荷兰失业总人口的40％。这样推算,总失业人口大概是600 000多一点。因此B项是正确的。

27．[答案]C

[解析]见原文："We study for jobs that don't exist."我们为根本不存在的工作而学习。联系上下文,本文讨论的中心议题是欧洲青年人的失业问题。因此即使是正在上学的年轻人也担心自己毕业后找不到工作。这也正是这句话的真正意思。C项与这一意思相同,是正确答案。

28．[答案]A

[解析]联系上下文可知,这些来自第三世界国家的打工者在那个年代(in the years of prosperity)受到欧洲国家的欢迎。那么"那个年代"肯定是经济上比较繁荣的时代。因为只有经济繁荣,产业对劳动力的需求才会增大。来自第三世界国家的打

工者才会受到欢迎。由此可以推知 prosperity 在此处的意思应该是经济上的繁荣。A项表达了这一意思,因此是正确答案。

29.[答案]B

[解析]B项意为"在西欧,外来打工者有40%失业"。这种说法在原文找不到与之相符的内容,属于文中未涉及的细节,因此不能妄下结论。所以此项内容不正确,符合题目要求,是正确答案。A项摇滚歌曲《没有未来》表达了欧洲青年的失望情绪。联系上文(第四段)"The bitter disappointment long expressed by British youth is spreading across the Continent",英国青年人长期以来表达的这种剧烈的失望正向整个欧洲大陆蔓延。因此说这首歌是欧洲青年失望情绪的一种表达。因此 A 项的内容是正确,不符题意。C项欧洲青年担心未来会有一场新的世界大战。此暗示可以从第四段中找:"... the possibility of nuclear war have clouded European youths' confidence in the future." D项失业的普遍性是欧洲青年未意料到的。从文中的第七段可以找到该意思的暗示。

30.[答案]C

[解析]原文第四段开头告诉读者:英国青年人长期以来表达的这种剧烈的失望正向整个欧洲大陆蔓延。这说明英国青年最先表达他们对没有工作的失望。C项符合这一说法,是正确答案。

Model Test 5

1. [答案]Y

[解析]本题问"无论主人的阶层高低,狗对他们的主人都很忠诚"这一说法是否正确。文章第一段第三句指出:"Class distinctions between people have no part in a dog's life. It can be a faithful companion to either rich or poor."主人的阶层对狗的生活没有影响,无论穷人、富人,狗都是他们忠诚的伙伴。这与题干相符,因此本题正确。

2. [答案]N

[解析]本题问"由于对主人忠诚,最近,狗受到所有人的欢迎"这一说法是否正确。文章第五段第一句明确指出:"Dogs are not always well thought of, however. In recent years dogs in the city have been in the center of controversy.""controversy"意为"争论,矛盾",说明狗并不是受到一致的欢迎,因此本题错误。

3. [答案]Y

[解析]本题问"虽然狗总是被单独关着,但它们还是喜欢和一群狗呆在一起"这一说法是否正确。文章第三节"The Dog Family"第一段第二句明确指出:"Dogs have retained the urge to be with the pack. This is why they do not like to be left alone for long.""pack"意为"群体",说明此句这与题干相符,因此本题正确。

4. [答案]NG

[解析]本题问"狗可以帮助人类照看孩子"这一说法是否正确。文中并未提到这一点。

5. [答案]Y

[解析]本题问"驯狗的最佳时间是在狗饿的时候,因为这样主人可以用食物来引诱狗听从主人的命令"这一说法是否正确。文章第四节"Dog Training"第三段明确指出:"A training session is best begun when the puppy is hungry because it is more alert at that time. Also, the owner can reinforce the dog's correct responses to commands with a dog biscuit or meat *tidbit*(少量的精美事物). The hungry dog is more apt to associate the correct performance of a task with a food reward..."这恰恰与题干相符,因此本题正确。

6. [答案]N

[解析]本题问"狗的主人应尽早用手势教狗明白'no'的意思"这一说法是否正确。文章第四节"Dog Training"第六段第一句明确指出"...but do teach it the meaning of 'no' at an earlier age",这与题干相符,因此本题正确。

7. [答案]N

[解析]本题问"如果训练时,狗的配合不好,训练者应该坚定、更严厉地给出指令"这一说法是否正确。文章最后一段明确指出:"If this is necessary, be firm but accompany the command with a friendly hand gesture."说明指令可以更友好一些,这恰恰与题干有矛盾,因此本题错误。

8.[答案]prehistoric

[解析]文章第三节"The Dog Family"第三段第一句指出:"Dogs have been with humans since prehistoric times."

9.[答案]guard dogs

[解析]文章第四节"Dog Training"第一段第一句指出:"Dogs are trained as guard dogs in peacetime by the United States Army and other military services."

10.[答案]after

[解析]文章倒数第二段第一句指出"To teach the command 'stay', work with the puppy after it has learned to sit."

Part II　Reading Comprehension(Reading in Depth)

Section A

11.[答案]G

[解析]此处需要一个动词,influence 意为"影响"。句意为:植物真的可以影响人类历史的进程。

12.[答案]M

[解析]此处需要一个副词,vitally 意为"决定性地,关键地"。句意为:几千年来,小麦对人类的重要性是决定性的。

13.[答案]D

[解析]living habits 意为"生活习惯",句意为:……我们祖先的生活习惯改变了。

14.[答案]K

[解析]in search of 意为"寻找",固定搭配。句意为:……寻找野外可以吃的动植物。

15.[答案]F

[解析]edible 意为"可食用的"。句意为:……寻找野外可以吃的动植物。

16.[答案]B

[解析]cultivated 意为"被种植",此处需要一个过去分词表示被动。句意为:……小麦可以被种植。

17.[答案]O

[解析]settlements 意为"居住地"。build settlements 为固定搭配。句意为:……如果他们能建造居住地。

18.[答案]E

[解析]harvested 意为"被收获",此处需要一个过去分词表示被动。harvest 专指收

77

获庄稼。句意为:小麦是一种种植简单的作物,然后收获,储备以便冬季食用。

19.[答案]J

[解析]more than 意为"多于"。句意为:……小麦比其他食物更带来了文明的发展。

20.[答案]L

[解析]civilization 意为"文明"。句意为:……小麦比其他食物更带来了文明的发展。

Section B

Passage One

21.[答案]D

[解析]文章开头第一句话提到:"One phase of the business cycle is the expansion phase."扩展阶段是商业循环周期中的一个阶段。文章讨论了在这个阶段工商业的迅速扩展和膨胀。文中提到:"However, a time comes when this phase reaches a peak and stops spiraling upward. This is the ending of the expansion."当这一阶段发展到一定的极点时,向上发展的势头就完全停止了,这就是扩展阶段的结束。根据逻辑推理,事物的发展在到达一个高潮之后就开始慢慢回落,商业也是如此。因此,可以推断,下一段内容就很自然地过渡到商业周期中的另一个阶段,衰退阶段。D 项与此意相同,是正确答案。

22.[答案]D

[解析]本短文讨论了商业周期中的一个阶段——扩展阶段。在这个阶段,工商业迅速发展,社会经济和生活水平不断提高。因此,可以说,这个阶段是社会发展的大好时光。A 项意为"商业循环周期",用于此题目过大,因为本文只讨论了其中一个阶段。B 项意为"恢复阶段",用于此题目过于片面。因为按文中所述,它只是扩展阶段中的一个分阶段。C 项意为"扩展的社会",不符合文章表达的内容,因为文章中只涉及社会生活的一个方面——工商业。D 项体现了这一意思,是正确答案。

23.[答案]A

[解析]见原文:"As one part of the economy develops, other parts are affected."当经济的一个环节发展时,其他环节就会受其影响。作者还以汽车工业的发展为例,汽车工业的发展导致了玻璃钢和橡胶工业的发展,同时带动了公路建设的发展等等。这说明了一种行业的繁荣发展,可以从其他许多行业中得到反映。A 项与此说法相同,符合题意,B 项会呈螺旋式地向上发展,与文意不符。文中已指出,当繁荣达到一定的极点时,它就会停止向上发展。C 项会对钢铁工业产生影响,用于此处不知所云。因为不是所有的行业繁荣都会对钢铁工业产生影响。D 项会突然停止,与文中意思不符。原文中说(末尾处):"This prosperity period may continue to rise ..."这种繁荣的时期还会继续发展。

24.[答案]B

[解析]本题题意是:下列各项中哪种工业能较好地体现扩展阶段? A项玩具;B项机械工具;C项粮食;D项农业。不难看出玩具、粮食、农业的发展都离不开机械工具。实际上,几乎所有的生产企业都与机器工具分不开。因此机械工具行业的发展更能较好地显示扩展阶段。由此,B项符合题意,是正确答案。

25.[答案]B

[解析]见原文:"There is an ever increasing optimism about the future of economic growth."人们对未来的经济增长持一种将不断提高的乐观态度。这说明人们对未来充满信心。因此B项是正确答案。

Passage Two

26.[答案]C

[解析]见原文第一句话:"The Ordinance of 1784 is most significant historically because it embodied the principle that new states should be formed from the western region and admitted to the Union on an equal basis with the original commonwealths."1784 的法令具有最为重要的历史意义,因为它体现了这样一个原则:新的州应当在西部领土建立,而且应当在平等的基础上加入最初的联邦。也就是说新成立的州和最初成立的州享有同等的权利。C项体现了这一观点,符合题意,是正确答案。A项新加入联邦的州和最初的几个州的数量相同,文中未提及。B项联邦应把西部地区建成附属州,明显与文意不符。D项广大西部地区应当分成 12 个州,文中未提及。

27.[答案]B

[解析]见原文:"This principle, which underlay the whole later development of the continental United States, was generally accepted by this time..."(1784)这个原则(即上文提到过的新州应当在平等的基础上加入最初建立的联邦)在这一时间(1784)得到了广泛的认可。B项答案与此意相同,是正确答案。

28.[答案]D

[解析]原文最后一句话提到:"What he dreamed of was an expanding union of self-governing commonwealths, joined as a group of peers."他(杰斐逊)的梦想是建立一个由各州平等加盟的广泛的自治联盟。由此可见杰斐逊强调"自治"和各州的"平等地位"是为了确保新成立的州的平等地位。因此,D项符合题意,是正确答案。

29.[答案]A

[解析]原文结尾提到:"He had no desire to break from the British Empire simply to establish an American one — in which the newer region should be subsidiary and tributary to the old."他(杰斐逊)不希望从大英帝国脱离出来后建立一个美洲自己的帝国在这样的帝国里,新地区附属于老地区。这就暗示在大英帝国内其他地方都是英国的附属地区。A项正确地表达了这个意思,符合题意,是正确答案。

30.[答案]B

[解析]文章开篇指出1784的法令具有重要的历史意义,因为它体现了州与州之间平等的原则。然后介绍了杰斐逊对于该法的确立所作的杰出贡献。可以看出,文章的中心议题是1784年所颁布的法令所体现的原则。因此,可以推想,文章的下一段也应该围绕这个中心议题展开。B项1784年法令的实施,和文章的中心议题紧密相关,很有可能是下一段将讨论的内容,符合题意。因此B项是正确答案。A项杰斐逊在弗吉尼亚的老家;C项英国殖民地向北美之外的扩张;D项弗吉尼亚的经济发展。三项均偏离了本文的主题。

Model Test 6

Part I Reading Comprehension（Skimming and Scanning）

1. ［答案］Y

   ［解析］文章中提到史蒂文的父母都酗酒，没有人管他，所以他自己不爱学习。

2. ［答案］Y

   ［解析］文章中提到怀特小姐是一个很美丽的老师，所以史蒂文见到她就喜欢她了。

3. ［答案］N

   ［解析］当怀特小姐发现史蒂文没有通过考试时，她并没有对他失望，而是鼓励他。

4. ［答案］N

   ［解析］在怀特小姐眼中，史蒂文是全班最聪明的学生。

5. ［答案］N

   ［解析］在怀特小姐的鼓励下，史蒂文开始好好学习，他改变了学校生活，但是家庭生活始终没有改变。

6. ［答案］NG

   ［解析］文章中没有提到史蒂文在军队中是否是一个优秀的士兵。

7. ［答案］Y

   ［解析］文章中提到史蒂文后来在一所大学里任兼职教授，继续鼓励年轻人。

8. ［答案］a radiant smile

   ［解析］在文章的倒数第五段可以找到答案。

9. ［答案］and that he could translate the things he learned into his own life

   ［解析］在文章的倒数第三段可以找到答案。

10. ［答案］might not have believed in themselves

   ［解析］在文章的倒数第二段可以找到答案。

Part II Reading Comprehension（Reading in Depth）

Section A

11. ［答案］A

   ［解析］此处要表达"为运动员服务的学校"，cater to "为……服务"。故选 A。

12. ［答案］F

   ［解析］此处要表达"Hunt 在这所学校里学习要更加独立"。independent "独立的"。故选 F。

13. ［答案］K

   ［解析］此处要表达"这种教育是专为那些经常在旅途中的运动员准备的"。on-the-go"在旅途中,在活动中"。故选 K。

14. [答案]M

[解析]此处要表达"被有一百多年历史的南部大学及学校联盟承认的 UMOHS。" accredited"公认的"。故选 M。

15. [答案]I

[解析]此处要表达"所有的课程资料、作业还有上交日期都是在线的"。assignment "作业,任务"。故选 I。

16. [答案]G

[解析]此处要表达"她不想耽误女儿的教育"。compromise "危及……"。故选 G。

17. [答案]J

[解析]此处要表达"普通学校不是我们的选择"。option"选择"。故选 J。

18. [答案]N

[解析]此处要表达"劳雷尔·斯普林斯学校的注册人数在过去四年以每年 35% 的速度增长"。enrollment "注册"。故选 N。

19. [答案]C

[解析]此处要表达"我曾经心存疑虑"。skeptic"怀疑的"。故选 C。

20. [答案]E

[解析]此处要表达"你不会碰到影响你一生的好老师"。inspire"激励"。故选 E。

Section B

Passage One

21. [答案]C

[解析]属情感态度题。从文章中 3 个地方"Ms Fiorina also reiterated why . . . forward for HP""One is to point out its advantages, which is what Ms Fiorina did this week"和 "Having spent the last several months . . . the power of this combination"可看出 Fiorina 对收购康柏的态度。故选 C。

22. [答案]A

[解析]属事实细节题。选项 B 对应的信息是"even if it was a bad idea to start with, abandoning it could be even worse";选项 C 对应的信息是"One is to point out its advantages";选项 D 对应的信息是"Part of the problem is that HP has no plan B"。从文章中可看出有支持这一方案的,也有反对的。故选 A。

23. [答案]D

[解析]属推理判断题。从文章中知道,惠普公司实际上没有可供选择的 B 方案,但它一定得使人感觉到它的强大和富有活力,而不能给人留下孤注一掷的印象,并且它的未来发展前景也不是取决于这项协议的。这样做的效果是会使合并计划更富有吸引力,也会使投资者重返董事会。因此,使人们相信惠普还有路可走,还有计可施,才能使收购计划顺利进行,而不再去想别的办法。故选 D。

24. [答案]B

   [解析]属事实细节题。原文对应的信息是"Part of the problem is that HP has no plan B"。实际上惠普公司已无计可施,只能仰仗收购计划,但它又不能表现出来。故选 B。

25. [答案]C

   [解析]属情感态度题。作者在阐述整个收购事件(其中包括公司内部股东的态度,收购带来的好处以及收购失败的坏处)时,态度是非常客观的。故选 C。

Passage Two

26. [答案]C

   [解析]属事实细节题。文中对应信息"Pfingst told his attorneys to go back over old murder and rape convictions and see if any unravel with newly developed DNA-testing tools"是对第二段第一句的补充说明。故选 C。

27. [答案]A

   [解析]属推理判断题。从上下文可以得知,实施"清白计划"就是使用先进的 DNA 技术来重新审理过去的案件当中可能存在的冤案、错案。故选 A。

28. [答案]D

   [解析]属猜词题。从第二段第一句话得知芬斯特可能是美国第一个实施非常独特的"清白计划"的人,因此他的做法很可能是令人感到吃惊的,从而可猜出该词的含义。故选 D。

29. [答案]B

   [解析]属推理判断题。从第一段和第二段给出的事例可以看出,芬斯特不愿放过任何一个犯罪的人,即便他的年龄还不算大;他也不愿使无辜者蒙冤,即便案件已经审理。故选 B。

30. [答案]C

   [解析]属推理判断题。正因为 "Pfingst's move works well",美国才又有"ten other counties are starting DNA audits",而且,"no budgets have been busted or prosecutors ousted",故选 C。

Model Test 7

11. ［答案］Y

　　［解析］在文章中提到根据世界的标准,美国人算是懒惰的。

12. ［答案］N

　　［解析］文章中提到在美国每周工作 48 小时以上的人占 18％。

13. ［答案］N

　　［解析］文中提到在过去的 40 年当中,美国人不断地增加他们休闲的时间。

14. ［答案］Y

　　［解析］文中提到美国女人在家里干的活要比以前少了。

15. ［答案］Y

　　［解析］文章中提到最近这些年在中国和印度人们的收入有所提高。

16. ［答案］NG

　　［解析］文章中没有提到这一点。

17. ［答案］Y

　　［解析］文章中提到全球的竞争需要人们投入更多的时间。

18. ［答案］those differences soon disappear

　　［解析］在文章的倒数第七段。

19. ［答案］we may have to work harder just to improve our living standard

　　［解析］在文章的倒数第四段。

20. ［答案］when he got a big order from the Transport Ministry

　　［解析］在文章的倒数第三段。

Part II　Reading Comprehension（Reading in Depth）

Section A

11. ［答案］D

　　［解析］此处要表达“借助技术,医生可以测试病人的遗传缺陷,并通过互联网很快将结果传遍全世界”。throughout“通过”。故选 D。

12. ［答案］K

　　［解析］此处要表达“上周比尔·克林顿总统向国会提交了一份病人权利法案的推论:医疗隐私权”。privacy“隐私权”。故选 K。

13. ［答案］G

　　［解析］此处要表达“从 2002 年开始,根据 2 月即将生效的法规,病人将有权规定

透露其个人医疗资料的条件"。divulged"泄露"。故选 G。

14. [答案]N

[解析]此处要表达"他们也可以了解哪些人曾看过他们的信息"。information"信息"。故选 N。

15. [答案]I

[解析]此句要表达"在促使美国人重新获得对自己的病历控制权方面迈出了前所未有的一步"。unprecedented"前所未有的"。故选 I。

16. [答案]A

[解析]此句要表达"虽然政府称这些法规尝试平衡消费者和医疗保健行业的需求"。attempt"尝试"。故选 A。

17. [答案]J

[解析]此句要表达"医生认为这些法规实际上是在破坏隐私权,因为其中一条规定允许管理式医疗保健计划(managed-care plan)在'开展医疗保健工作'时可以不经许可使用个人信息"。consent"许可,同意"。故选 J。

18. [答案]C

[解析]此句要表达"同时,保险公司也对这些法规持反对意见,他们认为这些法规很容易让他们惹上官司"。protested"抗议"。故选 C。

19. [答案]M

[解析]此句要表达"根据新法规的执行条例,联邦政府将加大对医疗保健行业的审查力度,他们对此也表示不满"。scrutiny"详细审查"。故选 M。

20. [答案]F

[解析]此句要表达"新法规的目标之一就是要让病人不再担心自己的隐私被泄露,从而鼓励他们对医生坦诚相告"。confidentiality"机密性"。故选 F。

Section B

Passage One

21. [答案]C

[解析]属情感态度题。从"There will, Kasparov says firmly, be no mistakes in this game"可看出 Kasparov 对比赛是充满信心的。故选 C。

22. [答案]A

[解析]属事实细节题。从"it's Kasparov's first public confrontation with computer technology"可知这是卡斯帕罗夫与电脑科技进行的首次公开对抗;从"This time, however, man and machine will work in harmony—on both sides"可知在这次比赛中人和机器将协调工作。这场比赛是卡斯帕罗夫通过计算机与全世界其他人的对抗赛,而不像是 1997 年进行的卡斯帕罗夫同"深蓝"计算机的比赛。故选 A。

23. [答案]D

[解析]属事实细节题。"beat (sb.) to a pulp"的意思是"把某人打得遍体鳞伤,打

85

个半死",在文中的意思是"把你我这样的业余无名小卒打得落花流水"。故选 D。

24.[答案]B

[解析]属情感态度题。从句子"And a few sniffles aren't likely to prevent the mighty Russian from beating amateur pawn pushers like you or me into a bloody pulp"可看出作者对卡斯帕罗夫的态度。故选 B。

25.[答案]C

[解析]属事实细节题。原文对应信息是"Kasparov, he says, thrives on pressure situations and may play less aggressive chess at a leisurely pace"。故选 C。

Passage Two

26.[答案]B

[解析]属事实细节题。原文对应信息是"...should not be allowed ... to sell them at cut-rate prices without getting permission first from the jeans maker",意思是"只有事先经过过牛仔裤生产商的同意才能打折销售"。是否只有生产商才能决定价格,我们不得而知。故选 B。

27.[答案]B

[解析]属推理判断题。文中提到问题的实质是"whether it is the job of the courts to help them do this",后又以古奇(Gucci)"saved itself not by resorting to the courts but by ending contracts with third-party suppliers, controlling its distribution better and opening its own stores. It is now hard to find cut-price Gucci anywhere"为例,说明它的成功并不是诉诸法庭,而是通过自身的努力和尝试。故选 B。

28.[答案]C

[解析]属猜词题。第二段开头提出了李维斯公司(Levi's)对特易购(Tesco)的指责,后又提出了特易购的反驳意见,前后两者之间的观点应该是相反的。从而可猜出该词的含义。故选 C。

29.[答案]D

[解析]属推理判断题。原文对应信息是最后一段。故选 D。

30.[答案]D

[解析]属情感态度题。作者没有任何偏颇地阐述整个事件。故选 D。

Model Test 8

Part I Reading Comprehension (Skimming and Scanning) (15 minutes)

1. [答案]N

[解析]关键词是"after 1955"。由此可以定位在原文"International Office"部分。在 "This office was set up in 1995 to provide a focal point for existing and intending international students of the University"这一句中,有 existing 一词,说明不是在 1995 年以后才招生,因此答案是 N。

2. [答案]NG

[解析]关键词是"free of charge"。在"International Office"部分查找原文,文中有 the orientation program,但没有提及费用问题,因此答案为 NG。

3. [答案]NG

[解析]关键词是"must"。一个中国学生或其他的外国学生到该校留学"一定"要加入学生会吗？到"Students' Union"部分去找,发现没有这种说法。因此答案为 NG。

4. [答案]N

[解析]关键词是"must"。先在"Medical Care"部分寻找原文。该部分第二句"Student residents on this campus or in the immediate surrounding area may therefore register with a doctor on campus"说明海外学生在哪里注册与他们的居住地有关,并且原文中是 "may...register with a doctor on campus"。因此答案为 N。

5. [答案]Y

[解析]关键词是"...is not covered by the university"。在"Medical Care"部分寻找原文。根据该部分第四句"由 UK 的 National health Service 提供免费医疗服务的条件"来看,当然不是由该大学负责,因此答案为 Y。

6. [答案]N

[解析]此题是关于牙科疾病由谁负担费用,答案仍然要在"Medical Care"部分寻找。根据该部分第二段括号中的说明(non-NHS practices charge more for treatment)可知 NHS practices 并不是不收费。因此答案是 N。

7. [答案]NG

[解析]关键词是"free"。文章最后一部分只提到"British Council organizes trips for overseas student",未提及费用,因此答案为 NG。

8. [答案]the Heathrow Airport

[解析]在文章的"International Office"部分可以找到答案。

9. [答案]Information and Advice Centers

[解析]该句在文章的"Information and Advice Centers"部分中提到。

10.[答案]trained counselors

[解析]在文章的"Counselors"部分可以找到答案。

Part II   Reading Comprehension（Reading in Depth）   (25 minutes)

Section A

11.[答案]J

[解析]由不定式 to 可知,空格处应填动词原形。由后一句的意思:每个军官都得到一些蘑菇,可推测几个人是一起分享蘑菇,所以选 share。

12.[答案]F

[解析]officer 是名词,需要形容词来修饰,所以该空应选一个形容词。由定语从句"who was afraid that the mushrooms might be poisonous"(害怕蘑菇会有毒)可知,该军官是很小心的,所以选 careful。

13.[答案]L

[解析]由 a 和形容词 pleasant,可知该空需填一个名词。该句的意思是:于是他们开始吃早餐,可知他们是在说蘑菇的味道,所以选 taste。

14.[答案]B

[解析]said 是动词,所以该空应选一个副词来修饰。由该空前后描写军官的句子"他们很奇怪和他们马上上车",可推测园丁是严肃地说狗死了,所以选 seriously。

15.[答案]D

[解析]由介词 into 可知该空需填一个名词。因为前文提到他们害怕蘑菇有毒,让狗先吃,而狗又死了,所以军官一定认为蘑菇有毒,他们就急忙去医院,所以选 hospital。

16.[答案]H

[解析]由介词 in 可知该空需填一个名词。由该句前部分可推测他们到医院是为了清除留在胃里的蘑菇,所以选 stomachs。

17.[答案]E

[解析]由不定式 to 可知该空需填一个动词原形。由后面的句子的谓语动词"解释和同意"可推测他们是在讨论蘑菇的毒性,所以选 discuss。

18.[答案] O

[解析]由助动词 did 可知该空需填一个动词原形。由前句意思可知,it 指的是dog,所以可推测军官是在问园丁狗在死的时候是否很痛苦,所以选 suffer。

19.[答案]N

[解析]由 a 和名词 death 可知该空需填一个形容词。并由前面的 escape 可知应选一个负面意义的词来修饰 death,所以选 painful。

20.[答案]G

[解析]由系动词 look 知该空应填一个形容词。由后面的句子意思"它是死于车

88

祸"可推测园丁对军官的话表示奇怪,所以选 surprised。

Section B

Passage One

21.[答案]B

[解析]重述题,主要依据是"The thought of the city's 24,000 cabbies bad-mouthing them to several dozen passengers a day has discouraged successive governments from trying to reform the archaic regulation"。

22.[答案]A

[解析]推理题,主要依据是"the archaic regulations that protect licensed taxis...ministers were relieved and the voters applauded"。

23.[答案]B

[解析]重述题,主要依据是"The mayor decided to smooth the path of change by giving cabbies the largest fare increase they have ever had"。

24.[答案]C

[解析]推理题,主要依据是"even many cab drivers believe that fares have risen too far, too fast...the price rises were appallingly handled"。

25.[答案]D

[解析]推理题,主要依据是"fare increase"或"price rises"。

Passage Two

26.[答案]A

[解析]在第一段的最后一句作者提到"People find jobs in an infinite number of ways"。所以应该选 A。numerous 是 an infinite number 的近义词。

27.[答案]B

[解析]在文章的第二段作者提到"others write to all sorts of places all over the country, and never seem to get a reply at all"。根据文章,选项 B 最符合原意。

28.[答案]B

[解析]文章明确指出,年轻人一直梦想着成为一名水手,所以只有选项 B 的说法是不正确的。

29.[答案]B

[解析]文章很随意、很轻松,并没有严密的逻辑性。B 项是最佳描述。

30.[答案]B

[解析]文章的最后一段说明,即使应聘的人给公司提意见也有可能得到一份很好的工作。

Part Ⅲ　历年真题及答案解析

2006 年 12 月 23 日大学英语四级考试 A 卷
COLLEGE ENGLISH TEST
- Band Four -

Part I   Writing（30 minutes）

Directions：
1.许多人喜欢在除夕夜观看春节晚会；
2.但有些人提出取消春节晚会；
3.我的看法。

Part II   Reading Comprehension
（Skimming and Scanning）（15 minutes）

Directions： *In this part，you will have 15 minutes to go over the passage quickly and answer the questions on **Answer Sheet 1**.*

For questions 1 ~ 7, mark

*Y（**for YES**）   if the statement agrees with the information given in the passage；*

*N（**for NO**）   if the statement contradicts the information given in the passage；*

*NG（**for NOT GIVEN**）   if the information is not given in the passage.*

For questions 8 ~ 10, complete the sentences with the information given in the passage.

Six Secrets of High-Energy People

There's an energy crisis in America, and it has nothing to do with fossil fuels. Millions of us get up each morning already weary over the day holds. "I just can't get started." People say. But it's not physical energy that most of us lack. Sure, we could all use extra sleep and a better diet. But in truth, people are healthier today than at any time in history. I can almost guarantee that if you long for more energy, the problem is not with your body.

What you're seeking is not physical energy. It's emotional energy. Yet, sad to say life sometimes seems designed to exhaust our supply. We work too hard. We have family obligations. We encounter emergencies and personal crises. No wonder so many of us suffer from emotional fatigue, a kind of utter exhaustion of the spirit.

And yet we all know people who are filled with joy, despite the unpleasant circumstances of their lives. Even as a child I observed people who were poor or disabled or ill, but who nonetheless faced life with optimism and vigor. Consider Laura Hillenbrand, who despite an extremely weak body wrote the best-seller *Seabiscuit*. Hillenbrand barely had enough physical energy to drag herself out of bed to write. But she was fueled by having a story she wanted to share. It was emotional energy that helped her succeed.

Unlike physical energy, which is finite and diminishes with age, emotional energy is unlimited and has nothing to do with genes or upbringing. So how do you get it? You can't simply tell yourself to be positive. You must take action. Here are six practical strategies that work.

1. Do something new

Very little that's new occurs in our lives. The impact of this sameness on our emotional energy is gradual, but huge: It's like a tire with a slow leak. You don't notice it at first, but eventually you'll get a flat. It's up to you to plug the leak—even though there are always a dozen reasons to stay stuck in your dull routines of life. That's where Maura, 36, a waitress, found herself a year ago.

Fortunately, Maura had a lifeline—a group of women friends who meet regularly to discuss their lives. Their lively discussions spurred Maura to make small but nevertheless life altering changes. She joined a gym in the next town. She changed her look with a short haircut and new black T-shirts. Eventually, Maura gathered the courage to quit her job and start her own business.

Here's a challenge: If it's something you wouldn't ordinarily do, do it. Try a dish you've never eaten. Listen to music you'd ordinarily tune out. You'll discover these small things add to your emotional energy.

2. Reclaim life's meaning

So many of my patients tell me that their lives used to have meaning, but that somewhere along the line things went state.

The first step in solving this meaning shortage is to figure out what you really care about, and then do something about it. A case in point is Ivy, 57, a pioneer in investment banking. "I mistakenly believed that all the money I made would mean something." she says. "But I feel lost, like a 22-year-old wondering what to do with her life." Ivy's solution? She started a program that shows Wall Streeters how to donate time and money to poor children. In the process, Ivy filled her life with meaning.

3. Put yourself in the fun zone

Most of us grown-ups are seriously fun-deprived. High-energy people have the same day-to-day work as the rest of us, but they manage to find something enjoyable in every situation. A real estate broker I know keeps herself amused on the job by mentally redecorating the houses she shows to clients. "I love imagining what even the most run-down house could look like withy a little tender loving care," she says. "It's a challenge—and the least desirable properties are usually the most fun."

We all define fun differently, of course, but I can guarantee this: If you put just a bit of it into your day, your energy will increase quickly.

4. Bid farewell to guilt and regret

Everyone's past is filled with regrets that still cause pain. But from an emotional energy point of view, they are dead weights that keep us from moving forward. While they can't merely be willed away, I do recommend you remind yourself that whatever happened is in the past, and nothing can change that. Holding on to the memory only allows the damage to continue into the present.

5. Make up your mind

Say you've been thinking about cutting your hair short. Will it look stylish—or too extreme?

You endlessly think it over. Having the decision hanging over your head is a huge energy drain.

Every time you can't decide, you burden yourself with alternatives. Quite thinking that you have to make the right decision; instead, make a choice and don't look back.

6. Give to get

Emotional energy has a kind of magical quality; the more you give, the more you get back. This is the difference between emotional and physical energy. With the latter, you have to get it to be able to give it. With the former, however, you get it by giving it.

Start by asking everyone you meet, "How are you?" as if you really want to know, then listen to the reply. Be the one who hears, most of us also need to smile more often. If you don't smile at the person you love first thing in the morning, you're sucking energy out of your relationship. Finally, help another person-and make the help real, concrete. Give a *massage* (按摩) to someone you love, or cook her dinner. Then, expand the circle to work. Try asking yourself what you'd do if your goal were to be helpful rather than efficient.

After all, if it's true that what goes around comes around, why not make sure that what's circulating around you is the good stuff?

注意:此部分试题请在答题卡 1 上作答。

1. The energy crisis in America discussed here mainly refers to a shortage of fossil fuels.

2. People these days tend to lack physical energy.

3. Laura Hillenbrand is an example cited to show how emotional energy can contribute to one's success in life.

4. The author believes emotional energy is inherited and genetically determined.

5. Even small changes people make in their lives can help increase their emotional energy.

6. They filled her life with meaning by launching a program to help poor children.

7. The real-estate broker the author knows is talented in home redecoration.

8. People holding on to sad memories of the past will find it difficult to _____.

9. When it comes to decision-making. One should make a quick choice without _____.

10. Emotional energy is in a way different from physical energy in that the more you give, _____.

Part III   Listening Comprehension（35 minutes）

Section A

Directions: *In this section, you will hear 8 short conversations and 2 long conversations. At the end of each conversation, one or more questions will be asked about what was said. Both the conversation and the questions will be spoken only once. After each question there will be a pause. During the pause, you must read the four choices marked A, B, C and D, and decide which is the best answer. Then marked the corresponding letter on* **Answer Sheet 2** *with a single line through the centre.*

注意:此部分试题请在答题卡 2 上作答。

11. A. Plan his budget carefully.   B. Give her more information.

    C. Ask someone else for advice.   D. Buy a gift for his girlfriend.

12. A. She'll have some chocolate cake.   B. She'll take a look at the menu.

    C. She'll go without dessert.   D. She'll prepare the dinner.

13. A. The man can speak a foreign language.

    B. The woman hopes to improve her English.

    C. The woman knows many different languages.

    D. The man wishes to visit many more countries.

14. A. Go to the library.   B. Meet the woman.

    C. See Professor Smith.   D. Have a drink in the bar.

15. A. She isn't sure when Professor Bloom will be back.

B. The man shouldn't be late for his class.

C. The man can come back sometime later.

D. She can pass on the message for the man.

16. A. He has a strange personality.   B. He's got emotional problems.

    C. His illness is beyond cure.   D. His behavior is hard to explain.

17. A. The tickets are more expensive than expected.

    B. The tickets are sold in advance at half price.

    C. It's difficult to buy the tickets on the spot.

    D. It's better to buy the tickets beforehand.

18. A. He turned suddenly and ran into a tree.

    B. He was hit by a fallen box from a truck.

    C. He drove too fast and crashed into a truck.

    D. He was trying to overtake the truck ahead of him.

Questions 19 to 21 are based on the conversation you have just heard.

19. A. To go boating on the St. Lawrence River.

    B. To go sightseeing in Quebec Province.

    C. To call on a friend in Quebec City.

    D. To attend a wedding in Montreal.

20. A. Study the map of Quebec Province.   B. Find more about Quebec Province.

    C. Brush up on her French.   D. Learn more about the local customs.

21. A. It's most beautiful in summer.

    B. It has many historical buildings.

    C. It was greatly expanded in the 18th century.

    D. It's the only French-speaking city in Canada.

Questions 22 to 25 are based on the conversation you have just heard.

22. A. It was about a little animal.

    B. It took her six years to write.

    C. It was adapted from a fairy tale.

    D. It was about a little girl and her pet.

23. A. She knows how to write best-selling novels.

    B. She can earn a lot of money by writing for adults.

    C. She is able to win enough support from publishers.

    D. She can make a living by doing what she likes.

24. A. The characters.   B. Her ideas.

    C. The readers.   D. Her life experiences.

25. A. She doesn't really know where they originated.

B. She mainly drew on stories of ancient saints.

C. They popped out of her childhood dreams.

D. They grew out of her long hours of thinking.

Section B

Directions: *In this section, you will hear 3 short passages. At the end of each passage, you will hear some questions. Both the passage and the questions will be spoken only once. After you hear a question, you must choose the best answer from the four choices marked A, B, C, and D. Then mark the corresponding letter on **Answer Sheet 2** with a single line through the center.*

注意：此部分试题请在答题卡 2 上作答。

Passage One

Questions 26 to 28 are based on the passage you have just heard.

26. A. Monitor students' sleep patterns.　　　　B. Help students concentrate in class.

　　C. Record students' weekly performance.　　D. Ask students to complete a sleep report.

27. A. Declining health.　　　　　　　　　　B. Lack of attention.

　　C. Loss of motivation.　　　　　　　　　D. Improper behavior.

28. A. They should make sure their children are always punctual for school.

　　B. They should ensure their children grow up in a healthy environment.

　　C. They should help their children accomplish high-quality work.

　　D. They should see to it that their children have adequate sleep.

Passage Two

Questions 29 to 32 are based on the passage you have just heard.

29. A. She stopped being a homemaker.　　　　B. She became a famous educator.

　　C. She became a public figure.　　　　　D. She quit driving altogether.

30. A. A motorist's speeding.　　　　　　　　B. Her running a stop sign.

　　C. Her lack of driving experience.　　　　D. A motorist's failure to concentrate.

31. A. Nervous and unsure of herself.　　　　B. Calm and confident of herself.

　　C. Courageous and forceful.　　　　　　D. Distracted and reluctant.

32. A. More strict training of women drivers.

　　B. Restrictions on cell phone use while driving.

　　C. Improved traffic conditions in cities.

　　D. New regulations to ensure children's safety.

Passage Three

Questions 33 to 35 are based on the passage you have just heard.

33. A. They haven't devoted as much energy to medicine as to space travel.

　　B. There are too many kinds of cold viruses for them to identify.

　　C. It is not economical to find a cure for each type of cold.

D. They believe people can recover without treatment.

34. A. They reveal the seriousness of the problem.

    B. They indicate how fast the virus spreads.

    C. They tell us what kind of medicine to take.

    D. They show our body is fighting the virus.

35. A. It actually does more harm than good.

    B. It causes damage to some organs of our body.

    C. It works better when combined with other remedies.

    D. It helps us to recover much sooner.

Section C

Directions: *In this section, you will hear a passage three times. When the passage is read for the first time, you should listen carefully for its general idea. When the passage is read for the second time, you are required to fill in the blanks numbered from 36 to 43 with the exact words you have just heard. For blanks numbered 44 to 46 you are required to fill in the missing information. For these blanks, you can either use the exact words you have just heard or write down the main points in your own words. Finally, when the passage is read for the third time, you should check what you have written.*

注意:此部分试题请在答题卡 2 上作答。

You probably have noticed that people express similar ideas in different ways depending on the situation they are in. This is very (36)＿＿＿＿＿. All languages have two general levels of (37)＿＿＿＿: a formal level and an informal level. English is no (38)＿＿＿＿. The difference in these two levels is the situation in which you use a (39)＿＿＿＿ level. Formal language is the kind of language you find in textbooks, (40)＿＿＿＿ books and in business letters. You would also use formal English in compositions and (41)＿＿＿＿ that you write in school. Informal language is used in conversation with (42)＿＿＿＿, family members and friends, and when we write (43)＿＿＿＿ notes or letters to close friends.

Formal language is different from informal language in several ways. First, formal language tends to be more polite. (44)＿＿＿＿＿＿＿＿＿＿＿＿＿＿＿＿＿＿＿. For example, I might say to a friend or a family member "Close the door, please". (45)＿＿＿＿＿＿＿＿＿＿＿＿＿＿＿＿＿＿＿.

Another difference between formal and informal language is some of the vocabulary. (46) ＿＿＿＿＿＿＿＿＿＿＿＿＿＿＿＿＿＿＿＿＿＿＿＿＿＿＿. Let's say that I really like soccer. If I am talking to my friend, I might say "I am just crazy about soccer", but if I were talking to my boss, I would probably say "I really enjoy soccer".

Part IV Reading Comprehension(Reading in Depth)
(25 minutes)

Section A

Directions: *In this section, there is a passage with ten blanks. You are required to select one word for each blank from a list of choices given in a word bank following the passage. Read the passage through carefully before making your choices. Each choice in the bank is identified by a letter. Please mark the corresponding letter for each item on **Answer Sheet 2** with a single line through the center. **You may not use any of the words in the blank more than once**.*

The flood of women into the job market boosted economic growth and changed U.S. society in many ways. Many in-home jobs that used to be done __47__ by women—ranging from family shopping to preparing meals to doing __48__ work—still need to be done by someone. Husbands and children now do some of these jobs, a __49__ that has changed the target market for many products. Or a working woman may face a crushing "poverty of time" and look for help elsewhere, creating opportunities for producers of frozen meals, child care centers, dry cleaners, financial services, and the like.

Although there is still a big wage __50__ between men and women, the income working women __51__ gives them new independence and buying power. For example, women now __52__ about half of all cars. Not long ago, many cars dealers __53__ women shoppers by ignoring them or suggesting that they come back with their husbands. Now car companies have realized that women are __54__ customers. It's interesting that some leading Japanese car dealers were the first to __55__ pay attention to women customers. In Japan, fewer women have jobs or buy cars — the Japanese society is still very much male-oriented. Perhaps it was the __56__ contrast with Japanese society that prompted American firms to pay more attention to women buyers.

注意:此部分试题请在答题卡 2 上作答。

A. scale	I. potential
B. retailed	J. gap
C. generate	K. voluntary
D. extreme	L. excessive
E. technically	M. insulted
F. affordable	N. purchase
G. situation	O. primarily
H. really	

Section B

Directions: *There are 2 passages in this section. Each passage is followed by some questions or unfinished statements. For each of them there are four choices marked A, B, C and D. You should decide on the best choice and mark the corresponding letter on* **Answer Sheet 2** *with a single line through the center.*

Passage One

Questions 57 to 61 are based on the following passage.

Reading new peaks of popularity in North America is Iceberg Water which is harvested from icebergs off the coast of Newfoundland, Canada.

Arthur von Wiesenberger, who carries the title Water Master, is one of the few water critics in North America. As a boy, he spent time in the larger cities of Italy, France and Switzerland, Where bottled water is consumed daily. Even then, he kept a water journal, noting the brands he liked best. "My dog could tell the difference between bottled and tap water." He says.

But is plain tap water all that bad? Not at all. In fact, New York's municipal water for more than a century was called the champagne of tap water and until recently considered among the best in the world in terms of both taste and purity. Similarly, a magazine in England found that tap water from the Thames River tasted better than several leading brands of bottled water that were 400 times more expensive.

Nevertheless, soft-drink companies view bottled water as the next battle-ground for market share—this despite the fact that over 25 percent of bottled water comes from tap water: PepsiCo's Aquafina and Coca-Cola's Dasani are both purified tap water rather than spring water.

As diners thirst for leading brands, bottlers and restaurateurs *salivate*(垂涎) over the profits. A restaurant's typical mark-up on wine is 100 to 150 percent, whereas on bottled water it's often 300 to 500 percent. But since water is much cheaper than wine, and many of the fancier brands aren't available in stores, most diners don't notice or care.

As a result, some restaurants are turning up the pressure to sell bottled water. According to an article in *The Wall Street Journal*, some of the more shameless tactics include placing attractive bottles on the table for a visual sell, listing brands on the menu without prices, and pouring bottled water without even asking the diners if they want it.

Regardless of how it's sold, the popularity of bottled water taps into our desire for better health, our wish to appear cultivated, and even a longing for lost purity.

注意:此部分试题请在答题卡 2 上作答。

57. What do we know about Iceberg Water from the passage?

A. It is a kind of iced water.

100

B. It is just plain tap water.

C. It is a kind of bottled water.

D. It is a kind of mineral water.

58. By saying "My dog could tell the difference between bottled and tap water" (Line 3 ~ 4, Para. 2), von wiesenberger wants to convey the message that _____.

A. plain tap water is certainly unfit for drinking

B. bottled water is clearly superior to tap water

C. bottled water often appeals more to dogs taste

D. dogs can usually detect a fine difference in taste

59. The "fancier brands" (Line 3, Para. 5) refers to _____.

A. tap water from the Thames River

B. famous wines not sold in ordinary stores

C. PepsiCo's Aquafina and Coca-Cola's Dasani

D. expensive bottled water with impressive names

60. Why are some restaurants turning up the pressure to sell bottled water?

A. Bottled water brings in huge profits.

B. Competition from the wine industry is intense.

C. Most diners find bottled water affordable.

D. Bottled water satisfied diners' desire to fashionable.

61. According to passage, why is bottled water so popular?

A. It is much cheaper than wine.

B. It is considered healthier.

C. It appeals to more cultivated people.

D. It is more widely promoted in the market.

Passage Two

Questions 62 to 66 are based on the following passage.

As we have seen, the focus of medical care in our society has been shifting from curing disease to preventing disease—especially in terms of changing our many unhealthy behaviors, such as poor eating habits, smoking, and failure to exercise. The line of thought involved in this shift can be pursued further. Imagine a person who is about the right weight , but does not eat very *nutritious*(有营养的) foods, who feels OK but exercises only occasionally, who goes to work every day, but is not an outstanding worker, who drinks a few beers at home most nights but does not drive while drunk , and who has no chest pains or abnormal blood counts, but sleeps a lot and often feels tired. This person is not ill. He may not even be at risk for any particular disease. But we can imagine that this person could be a lot healthier.

The field of medicine has not traditionally distinguished between someone who is merely "not ill" and someone who is in excellent health and pays attention to the body's special needs. Both types have simply been called "well". In recent years, however, some health specialists have begun to apply the terms "well" and "wellness" only to those who are actively striving to maintain and improve their health. People who are well are concerned with nutrition and exercise and they make a point of monitoring their body's condition. Most important, perhaps, people who are well take active responsibility for all matters related to their health. Even people who have a physical disease or *handicap* (缺陷) may be "well", in this new sense, if they make an effort to maintain the best possible health they can in the face of their physical limitations. "Wellness" may perhaps best be viewed not as a state that people can achieve, but as an ideal that people can strive for. People who are well are likely to be better able to resist disease and to fight disease when it strikes. And by focusing attention on healthy ways of living, the concept of wellness can have a beneficial impact on the ways in which people face the challenges of daily life.

注意:此部分试题请在答题卡 2 上作答。

62. Today medical care is placing more stress on _____.

A. keeping people in a healthy physical condition

B. monitoring patients' body functions

C. removing people's bad living habits

D. ensuring people's psychological well-being

63. In the first paragraph, people are reminded that _____.

A. good health is more than not being ill

B. drinking, even if not to excess, could be harmful

C. regular health checks are essential to keeping fit

D. prevention is more difficult than cure

64. Traditionally, a person is considered "well" if he _____.

A. does not have any unhealthy living habits

B. does not have any physical handicaps

C. is able to handle his daily routines

D. is free from any kind of disease

65. According to the author, the true meaning of "wellness" is for people _____.

A. to best satisfy their body's special needs

B. to strive to maintain the best possible health

C. to meet the strictest standards of bodily health

D. to keep a proper balance between work and leisure

66. According to what the author advocates, which of the following groups of people would be considered healthy?

A. People who have strong muscles as well as slim figures.

B. People who are not presently experiencing any symptoms of disease.

C. People who try to be as possible, regardless of their limitations.

D. People who can recover from illness even without seeking medical care.

Part V Cloze (15 minutes)

Directions: *There are 20 blanks in the following passage. For each blank there are four choices marked A, B, C and D on the right side of the paper. You should choose the ONE that best fits into the passage. Then mark the corresponding letters on **Answer Sheet 2** with a single line through the center.*

注意：此部分试题请在答题卡 2 上作答。

Language is the most astonishing behavior in the animal kingdom. It is the species-typical behavior that sets humans completely __67__ from all other animals. Language is a means of communication, __68__ it is much more than that. Many animals can __69__. The dance of the honeybee communicates the location of flowers __70__ other members of the *hive*(蜂群). But human language permits communication about anything, __71__ things like *unicorn*(独角兽)that have never existed. The key __72__ in the fact that the units of meaning, words, can be __73__ together in different ways, according to __74__, to communicate different meanings.

Language is the most important learning we do. Nothing __75__ humans so much as our ability to communicate abstract thoughts, __76__ about the university the mind, love, dreams, or ordering a drink. It is an immensely complex __77__ that we take for granted. Indeed, we are not aware of most __78__ of our speech and understanding. Consider what happens when one person is speaking to __79__. The Speaker has to translate thoughts into __80__ language. Brain imaging studies suggest that the time from thoughts to the __81__ of speech is extremely fast. Only 0.04 seconds! The listener must hear the sounds to __82__ out what the speaker means. He must use the sounds of speech to __83__ the words spoken., understand the pattern of __84__ of the words (sentences), and finally __85__ the meaning. This takes somewhat longer, a minimum of about 0.5 seconds. But __86__ started, it is of course a continuous process.

67. A. apart   B. off   C. up   D. down

68. A. so   B. but   C. or   D. for

69. A. transfer   B. transmit   C. convey   D. communicate

70. A. to   B. from   C. over   D. on

71. A. only   B. almost   C. even   D. just

72. A. stays   B. situates   C. hides   D. lies

103

73. A. stuck   B. strung   C. rung   D. consisted

74. A. rules   B. scales   C. laws   D. standards

75. A. combines   B. contains   C. defines   D. declares

76. A. what   B. whether   C. while   D. if

77. A. prospect   B. progress   C. process   D. produce

78. A. aspects   B. abstracts   C. angles   D. assumptions

79. A. anybody   B. another   C. other   D. everybody

80. A. body   B. gesture   C. written   D. spoken

81. A. growing   B. fixing   C. beginning   D. building

82. A. put   B. take   C. draw   D. figure

83. A. identify   B. locate   C. reveal   D. discover

84. A. performance   B. organization   C. design   D. layout

85. A. prescribe   B. justify   C. utter   D. interpret

86. A. since   B. after   C. once   D. until

Part VI Translation (*5 minutes*)

Directions: *Complete the sentences by translating into English the Chinese given in brackets.*
*Please write your translation on **Answer Sheet 2**.*

注意:此部分试题请在答题卡 2 上作答。

87. Specialists in intercultural studies says that it is not easy to _____(适应不同文化中的生活).

88. Since my childhood I have found that _____(没有什么比读书对我更有吸引力).

89. The victim _____(本来有机会活下来)if he had been taken to hospital in time.

90. Some psychologists claim that people _____(出门在外时可能会感到孤独).

91. The nation's population continues to rise _____(以每年 1 200 万人的速度).

2006年12月23日大学英语四级考试A卷参考答案

COLLEGE ENGLISH TEST(Band Four)

Part I Writing

参考范文

The approach of the Chinese Lunar New Year poses a national issue concerning the necessity of holding the CCTV Spring Festival Gala. Its established status is being challenged by a growing number of people, especially by younger generations. It is increasingly difficult to cater for all tastes.

Some individuals deem that it should be canceled or replaced by other programs. These young people focus their attention on other forms of celebration instead of immersing themselves in TV. Despite that, the majority of mid-aged people and senior citizens uphold the importance of the traditional performance. The most striking feature of this gala is its traditionally close link with ordinary people's lives. Most of people view this gala as an annual staple on the traditional Chinese Spring Festival Eve. They all have a restless night and glue their eyes on the television.

I am not supportive of the view that the grand gala should be abandoned. Undoubtedly, it plays a vital role in the celebration of Chinese New Year. To increase its appeal and meet young adults' need, the upcoming performance should invite some big names including super stars from Hongkong and Taiwan. We are all eagerly anticipating this unforgettable evening show.

Part II Reading Comprehension (Skimming and Scanning)

1. N 2. N 3. Y 4. N 5. Y 6. Y 7. NG

8. move forward 9. looking back 10. the more you get back

Part III Listening Comprehension

Section A

11. B. Give her more information.

12. C. She'll go without dessert.

13. A. The man can speak a foreign language.

14. C. See Prof. Smith.

15. D. She can pass on the message for the man.

16. B. He's got emotional problems.

17. D. It's better to buy the tickets beforehand.

18. A. He turned suddenly and ran into a tree.

19. D. To attend a wedding in Montreal.

20. C. Brush up on her French.

21. B. It has many historical buildings.

22. A. It was about a little animal.

23. D. She can make a living by doing what she likes.

24. B. Her ideas.

25. A. She doesn't really know where they originated.

Section B

26. C. Record students' weekly performance.

27. B. Lack of attention.

28. D. They should see to it that their children have adequate sleep.

29. C. She became a public figure.

30. D. A motorist's failure to concentrate.

31. A. Nervous and unsure of herself.

32. B. Restrictions on cell phone use while driving.

33. B. There are too many kinds of cold viruses for them to identify.

34. D. They show our body is fighting the virus.

35. A. It actually does more harm than good.

Section C

36. natural   37. usage   38. exception   39. particular

40. reference   41. essays   42. colleagues   43. personal

44. What we may find interesting is that it usually takes more words to be polite

45. But to a stranger, I probably would say, "Would you mind closing the door?"

46. There are bound to be some words and phrases that belong in formal language and others that are informal.

Part IV   Reading Comprehension (Reading in Depth)

Section A

47. O. primarily   48. K. voluntary   49. G. situation   50. J. gap   51. C. generate

52. N. purchase   53. M. insulted   54. I. potential   55. H. really   56. D. extreme

Section B

57. C. It is a kind of bottled water.

58. B. bottled water is clearly superior to tap water

59. D. expensive bottled water with impressive names

60. A. Bottled water brings in huge profits.

61. B. It is considered healthier

62. C. removing people's bad living habits

63. A. good health is more than not being ill

64. D. is free from any kind of disease

65. B. to strive to maintain the best possible health

66. C. People who try to be as healthy as possible, regardless of their limitations.

Part V   Cloze

67. A. apart	68. B. but	69. D. communicate	70. A. to	71. C. even
72. D. lies	73. B. strung	74. A. rules	75. C. defines	76. B. whether
77. C. process	78. A. aspects	79. B. another	80. D. spoken	81. D. building
82. D. figure	83. A. identify	84. B. organization	85. D. interpret	86. C. once

Part VI   Translation

87. adapt to the life in different cultures

88. nothing is more attractive / interesting / appealing to me than reading

89. might / would / could have survived / been alive

90. may feel lonely when they are away from home

91. at a / the rate of 12 million per year

2006 年 12 月 23 日大学英语
四级考试 A 卷听力原文
COLLEGE ENGLISH TEST(Band Four)

Part III   Listening Comprehension

Section A

11. M: Christmas is around the corner. And I'm looking for a gift for my girlfriend. Any suggestions?

   W: Well you have to tell me something about your girlfriend first. Also, what's your budget?

   Q: What does the woman want the man to do?

12. M: What would you like for dessert? I think I'll have apple pie and ice cream.

   W: The chocolate cake looks great, but I have to watch my weight. You go ahead and get yours.

   Q: What would the woman most probably do?

13. W: Having visited so many countries, you must be able to speak several different langua-

ges.

M: I wish I could. But Japanese and, of course English are the only languages I can speak.

Q: What do we learn from the conversation?

14. M: Professor Smith asked me to go to his office after class. So it's impossible for me to make it to the bar at ten.

W: Then it seems that we'll have to meet an hour later at the library.

Q: What will the man do first after class?

15. M: It's already 11 now. Do you mean I ought to wait until Mr. Bloom comes back from the class?

W: Not really. You can just leave a note. I'll give it to her later.

Q: What does the woman mean?

16. M: How is John now? Is he feeling any better?

W: Not yet. It still seems impossible to make him smile. Talking to him is really difficult and he gets upset easily over little things.

Q: What do we learn about John from the conversation?

17. M: Do we have to get the opera tickets in advance?

W: Certainly. Tickets at the door are usually sold at a higher price.

Q: What does the woman imply?

18. M: The taxi driver must have been speeding.

W: Well, not really. He crashed into the tree because he was trying not to hit a box that had fallen off the truck ahead of him.

Q: What do we learn about the taxi driver?

Conversation One

W: Hey, Bob, guess what? I'm going to visit Quebec next summer. I'm invited to go to a friend's wedding. But while I'm there I'd also like to do some sightseeing.

M: That's nice, Shelly. But do you mean the province of Quebec, or Quebec City?

W: I mean the province. My friend's wedding is in Montreal. I'm going there first. I'll stay for five days. Is Montreal the capital city of the province?

M: Well, Many people think so because it's the biggest city. But it's not the capital. Quebec City is. But Montreal is great. The Saint Royal River runs right through the middle of the city. It's beautiful in summer.

W: Wow, and do you think I can get by in English? My French is OK, but not that good. I know most people there speak French, but can I also use English?

M: Well, People speak both French and English there. But you'll hear French most of the time. And all the street signs are in French. In fact, Montreal is the third largest French speaking city in the world. So you'd better practice your French before you go.

W: Good advice. What about Quebec City? I'll visit a friend from college who lives there now. What's it like?

M: It's a beautiful city, very old. Many old buildings have been nicely restored. Some of them were built in the 17th or 18th centuries. You'll love there.

W: Fantastic. I can't wait to go.

19. What's the woman's main purpose of visiting Quebec?

20. What does the man advise the woman to do before the trip?

21. What does the man say about the Quebec City?

Conversation Two

M: Hi, Miss Rowling, how old were you when you started to write? And what was your first book?

W: I wrote my first Finnish (finished) story when I was about six. It was about a small animal, a rabbit, I mean. And I've been writing ever since?

M: Why did you choose to be an author?

W: If someone asked me how to achieve happiness. Step one would be finding out what you love doing most. Step two would be finding someone to pay you to do this. I consider myself very lucky indeed to be able to support myself by writing

M: Do you have any plans to write books for adults?

W: My first two novels were for adults. I suppose I might write another one. But I never really imagine a target audience when I'm writing. The ideas come first. So it really depends on the ideas that grasp me next.

M: Where did the ideas for the "Harry Potter" books come from?

W: I've no ideas where the ideas came from. And I hope I'll never find out. It would spoil my excitement if it turned out. I just have a funny wrinkle on the surface of my brain, which makes me think about the invisible train platform.

M: How did you come up with the names of your characters?

W: I invented some of them. But I also collected strange names. I've got one from ancient saints, maps, dictionaries, plants, war memoirs and people I met.

M: Oh, you are really resourceful.

22. What do we learn from the conversation about Miss Rowling's first book?

23. Why does Miss Rowling consider her so very lucky?

24. What dictates Miss Rowling's writing?

25. According to Miss Rowling where did she get the ideas for the Harry Porter books?

Section B

Passage One

Reducing the amount of sleep students get at night has a direct impact on their performance at school during the day. According to classroom teachers, elementary and middle school students who stay up late exhibit more learning and attention problems. This has been shown by Brown Medical School and Bradley Hospital research. In the study, teachers were not told the amount of sleep students received when completing weekly performance reports, yet they rated the students who had received eight hours or less as having the most trouble recalling all the material, learning new lessons and completing high-quality work. Teachers also reported that these students had more difficulty paying attention. The experiment is the first to ask teachers to report on the effects of sleep deficiency in children. Just staying up late can cause increased academic difficulty and attention problems for otherwise healthy, well-functioning kids, said Garharn Forlone, the study's lead author. So the results provide professionals and parents with a clear message: when a child is having learning and attention problems, the issue of sleep has to be taken into consideration. "If we don't ask about sleep, and try to improve sleep patterns in kids' struggling academically, then we aren't doing our job," Forlone said. For parents, he said, the message is simple, "getting kids to bed on time is as important as getting them to school on time".

26. What were teachers told to do in the experiment?

27. According to the experiment, what problem can insufficient sleep cause in students?

28. What message did the researcher intend to convey to parents?

Passage Two

Patricia Pania never wanted to be a public figure. All she wanted to be was a mother and home-maker. But her life was turned upside down when a motorist, distracted by his cell phone, ran a stop sign and crashed into the side of her car. The impact killed her 2-year-old daughter. Four months later, Pania reluctantly but courageously decided to try to educate the public and to fight for laws to ban drivers from using cell phones while a car is moving. She wanted to save other children from what happened to her daughter. In her first speech, Pania got off to a shaky start. She was visibly trembling and her voice was soft and uncertain. But as she got into her speech, a dramatic transformation took place. She stopped shaking and spoke with a strong voice. For the rest of her talk, she was a forceful and compelling speaker. She wanted everyone in the audience to know what she knew without having to learn it from a personal tragedy. Many in the audience were moved to tears and to action. In subsequent presentations, Pania gained reputation as a highly effective speaker. Her appearance on a talk show was broadcast three times, transmitting her message to over 40 million people. Her campaign increased public awareness of the problem, and prompted over 300 cities and several states to consider restrictions on cell phone use.

29. What was the significant change in Patricia Pania's life?

30. What had led to Pania's personal tragedy?

31. How did Pania feel when she began her first speech?

32. What could be expected as a result of Pania's efforts?

Passage Three

Many people catch a cold in the spring time or fall. It makes us wonder if scientists can send a man to the moon. Why can't they find a cure for the common cold? The answer is easy. There're actually hundreds of kinds of cold viruses out there. You never know which one you will get, so there isn't a cure for each one. When a virus attacks your body, your body works hard to get rid of it. Blood rushes to your nose and causes a blockade in it. You feel terrible because you can't breathe well, but your body is actually eating the virus. Your temperature rises and you get a fever, but the heat of your body is killing the virus. You also have a running nose to stop the virus from getting into your cells. You may feel miserable, but actually your wonderful body is doing everything, it can kill the cold. Different people have different remedies for colds. In the United States and some other countries, for example, people might eat chicken soup to feel better. Some people take hot bath and drink warm liquids. Other people take medicines to relieve various symptoms of colds. There was one interesting thing to note. Some scientists say taking medicines when you have a cold is actually bad for you. The virus stays in you longer, because your body doesn't develop a way to fight it and kill it.

33. According to the passage, why haven't scientists found a cure for the common cold?

34. What does the speaker say about the symptoms of the common cold?

35. What do some scientists say about taking medicines for the common cold, according to the passage?

2007 年 6 月 23 日大学英语四级考试 A 卷
COLLEGE ENGLISH TEST
– Band Four –

Part I Writing (*30 minutes*)

Directions:

1. 本社团的主要活动内容;
2. 参加本社团的好处;
3. 如何加入本社团。

Part II Reading Comprehension
(*Skimming and Scanning*) (*15 minutes*)

Directions: *In this part, you will have 15 minutes to go over the passage quickly and answer the questions on **Answer Sheet 1**.*

For questions 1 ~ 7, mark

Y (*for YES*)   *if the statement agrees with the information given in the passage;*

N (*for NO*)   *if the statement contradicts the information given in the passage;*

NG (*for NOT GIVEN*)   *if the information is not given in the passage.*

For questions 8 ~ 10, complete the sentences with the information given in the passage.

Protect Your Privacy When Job-hunting Online

Identity theft and identity fraud are terms used to refer to all types of crime in which someone wrongfully obtains and uses another person's personal data in some way that involves fraud or deception, typically for economic gain.

The numbers associated with identity theft are beginning to add up fast these days. A recent General Accounting Office report estimates that as many as 750,000 Americans are victims of identity theft every year. And that number may be low, as many people choose not to report the crime even if they know they have been victimized.

Identity theft is "an absolute epidemic", states Robert Ellis Smith, a respected author and advocate of privacy. "It's certainly picked up in the last four or five years. It's worldwide. It affects everybody, and there's very little you can do to prevent it and, worst of all, you can't detect it until it's probably too late."

Unlike your fingerprints, which are unique to you and cannot be given to someone else for their use, your personal data, especially your social security number, your bank account or credit card number, your telephone calling card number, and other valuable identifying data, can be used, if they fall into the wrong hands, to personally profit at your expense. In the United States and Canada, for example, many people have reported that unauthorized persons have taken funds out of their bank or financial accounts, or in the worst cases, taken over their identities altogether, running up vast debts and committing crimes while using the victims' names. In many cases, a victim's losses may include not only out-of-pocket financial losses, but substantial additional financial costs associated with trying to restore his reputation in the community and correcting erroneous information for which the criminal is responsible.

According to the FBI, identity theft is the number one fraud committed on the Internet. So how do job seekers protect themselves while continuing to circulate their resumes online? The key to a successful online job search is learning to manage the risks. Here are some tips for staying safe while conducting a job search on the Internet.

1. Check for a privacy policy.

If you are considering posting your resume online, make sure the job search site you are considering has a privacy policy, like CareerBuilder.com. The policy should spell out how your information will be used, stored and whether or not it will be shared. You may want to think twice about posting your resume on a site that automatically shares your information with others. You could be opening yourself up to unwanted calls from *solicitors* (推销员).

When reviewing the site's privacy policy, you'll be able to delete your resume just as easily as you posted it. You won't necessarily want your resume to remain out there on the Internet once you land a job. Remember, the longer your resume remains posted on a job board, the more exposure, both positive and not-so-positive, it will receive.

2. Take advantage of site features.

Lawful job search sites offer levels of privacy protection. Before posting your resume, carefully consider your job search objectives and the level of risk you are willing to assume.

CareerBuilder.com, for example, offers three levels of privacy from which job seekers can choose. The first is standard posting. This option gives job seekers who post their resumes the most visibility to the broadest employer audience possible.

The second is *anonymous* (匿名的) posting. This allows job seekers the same visibility as those in the standard posting category without any of their contact information being displayed. Job seekers who wish to remain anonymous but want to share some other information may choose which pieces of contact information to display.

The third is private posting. This option allows a job seeker to post a resume without having it searched by employers. Private posting allows job seekers to quickly and easily apply for jobs that appear on CareerBuilder.com without retyping their information.

3. Safeguard your identity.

Career experts say that one of the ways job seekers can stay safe while using the Internet to search out jobs is to conceal their identities. Replace your name on your resume with a *generic* (泛指的) identifier, such as "Intranet Developer Candidate" or "Experienced Marketing Representative".

You should also consider eliminating the name and location of your current employer. Depending on your title, it may not be all that difficult to determine who you are once the name of your company is provided. Use a general description of the company such as "Major auto manufacturer" or "International packaged goods supplier".

If your job title is unique, consider using the generic equivalent instead of the exact title assigned by your employer.

4. Establish an email address for your search.

Another way to protect your privacy while seeking employment online is to open up an E-mail account specifically for your online job search. This will safeguard your existing E-mail box in the event someone you don't know gets hold of your E-mail address and shares it with others.

Using an E-mail address specifically for your job search also eliminates the possibility that you will receive unwelcome E-mails in your primary mailbox. When naming your new E-mail address, be sure that it doesn't contain references to your name or other information that will give away your identity. The best solution is an E-mail address that is relevant to the job you are seeking such as Salesmgr2004@provider.com.

5. Protect your references.

If your resume contains a section with the names and contact information of your references, take it out. There's no sense in safeguarding your information while sharing private contact information of your references.

6. **Keep** *confidential* （机密的） **information confidential**.

Do not, under any circumstances, share your social security, driver's license, and bank account numbers or other personal information, such as race or eye color. Honest employers do not need this information with an initial application. Don't provide this even if they say they need it in order to conduct a background check. This is one of the oldest tricks in the book — don't fall for it.

1. Robert Ellis Smith believes identity theft is difficult to detect and one can hardly do anything to prevent it.
2. In many cases, identity theft not only causes the victims' immediate financial losses but costs them a lot to restore their reputation.
3. Identity theft is a minor offence and its harm has been somewhat overestimated.
4. It is important that your resume not stay online longer than is necessary.
5. Of the three options offered by CareerBuilder.com in Suggestion 2, the third one is apparently most strongly recommended.
6. Employers require applicants to submit very personal information on background checks.
7. Applicants are advised to use generic names for themselves and their current employers when seeking employment online.
8. Using a special email address in the job search can help prevent you from receiving _____.
9. To protect your references, you should not post online their _____.
10. According to the passage, identity theft is committed typically for _____.

Part III   Listening Comprehension （35 minutes）

Section A

Directions: *In this section, you will hear 8 short conversations and 2 long conversations. At the end of each conversation, one or more questions will be asked about what was said. Both the conversation and the questions will be spoken only once. After each question there will be a pause. During the pause, you must read the four choices marked A, B, C and D, and decide which is the best answer. Then marked the corresponding letter on **Answer Sheet 2** with a single line through the centre.*

注意：此部分试题请在答题卡 2 上作答。

11. A. It could help people of all ages to avoid cancer.

    B. It was mainly meant for cancer patients.

    C. It might appeal more to viewers over 40.

D. It was frequently interrupted by commercials.

12. A. The man is fond of traveling.

B. The woman is a photographer.

C. The woman took a lot of pictures at the contest.

D. The man admires the woman's talent in writing.

13. A. The man regrets being absent-minded.

B. The woman saved the man some trouble.

C. The man placed the reading list on a desk.

D. The woman emptied the waste paper basket.

14. A. He quit teaching in June.

B. He has left the army recently.

C. He opened a restaurant near the school.

D. He has taken over his brother's business.

15. A. She seldom reads books from cover to cover.

B. She is interested in reading novels.

C. She only read part of the book.

D. She was eager to know what the book was about.

16. A. She was absent all week owing to sickness.

B. She was seriously injured in a car accident.

C. She called to say that her husband had been hospitalized.

D. She had been away from school to attend to her husband.

17. A. The speakers want to rent the Smiths' old house.

B. The man lives two blocks away from the Smiths.

C. The woman is not sure if she is on the right street.

D. The Smiths' new house is not far from their old one.

18. A. The man had a hard time finding a parking space.

B. The woman found they had got to the wrong spot.

C. The woman was offended by the man's late arrival.

D. The man couldn't find his car in the parking lot.

Questions 19 to 22 are based on the conversation you have just heard.

19. A. The hotel clerk had put his reservation under another name.

B. The hotel clerk insisted that he didn't make any reservation.

C. The hotel clerk tried to take advantage of his inexperience.

D. The hotel clerk couldn't find his reservation for that night.

20. A. A grand wedding was being held in the hotel.

B. There was a conference going on in the city.

116

C. The hotel was undergoing major repairs.

D. It was a busy season for holiday-makers.

21. A. It was free of charge on weekends.

B. It had a 15% discount on weekdays.

C. It was offered to frequent guests only.

D. It was 10% cheaper than in other hotels.

22. A. Demand compensation from the hotel.

B. Ask for an additional discount.

C. Complain to the hotel manager.

D. Find a cheaper room in another hotel.

Questions 23 to 25 are based on the conversation you have just heard.

23. A. An employee in the city council at Birmingham.

B. Assistant Director of the Admissions Office.

C. Head of the Overseas Students Office.

D. Secretary of Birmingham Medical School.

24. A. Nearly fifty percent are foreigners.

B. About fifteen percent are from Africa.

C. A large majority are from Latin America.

D. A small number are from the Far East.

25. A. She will have more contact with students.

B. It will bring her capability into fuller play.

C. She will be more involved in policy-making.

D. It will be less demanding than her present job.

Section B

Directions: *In this section, you will hear 3 short passages. At the end of each passage, you will hear some questions. Both the passage and the questions will be spoken only once. After you hear a question, you must choose the best answer from the four choices marked A, B, C and D. Then mark the corresponding letter on **Answer Sheet 2** with a single line through the center.*

注意:此部分试题请在答题卡 2 上作答。

Passage One

Questions 26 to 28 are based on the passage you have just heard.

26. A. Her parents thrived in the urban environment.

B. Her parents left Chicago to work on a farm.

C. Her parents immigrated to America.

D. Her parents set up an ice-cream store.

27. A. He taught English in Chicago.

B. He was crippled in a car accident.

C. He worked to become an executive.

D. He was born with a limp.

28. A. She was fond of living an isolated life.

B. She was fascinated by American culture.

C. She was very generous in offering help.

D. She was highly devoted to her family.

Passage Two

Questions 29 to 32 are based on the passage you have just heard.

29. A. He suffered a nervous breakdown.

B. He was wrongly diagnosed.

C. He was seriously injured.

D. He developed a strange disease.

30. A. He was able to talk again.

B. He raced to the nursing home.

C. He could tell red and blue apart.

D. He could not recognize his wife.

31. A. Twenty-nine days.

B. Two and a half months.

C. Several minutes.

D. Fourteen hours.

32. A. They welcomed the publicity in the media.

B. They avoided appearing on television.

C. They released a video of his progress.

D. They declined to give details of his condition.

Passage Three

Questions 33 to 35 are based on the passage you have just heard.

33. A. For people to share ideas and show farm products.

B. For officials to educate the farming community.

C. For farmers to exchange their daily necessities.

D. For farmers to celebrate their harvests.

34. A. By bringing an animal rarely seen on nearby farms.

B. By bringing a bag of grain in exchange for a ticket.

C. By offering to do volunteer work at the fair.

D. By performing a special skill at the entrance.

35. A. They contribute to the modernization of American farms.

B. They help to increase the state governments' revenue.

C. They provide a stage for people to give performances.

D. They remind Americans of the importance of agriculture.

Section C

Directions: *In this section, you will hear a passage three times. When the passage is read for the first time, you should listen carefully for its general idea. When the passage is read for the second time, you are required to fill in the blanks numbered from 36 to 43 with the exact words you have just heard. For blanks numbered from 44 to 46 you are required to fill in the missing information. For these blanks, you can either use the exact words you have just heard or write down the main points in your own words. Finally, when the passage is read for the third time, you should check what you have written.*

注意:此部分试题请在答题卡 2 上作答。

Students' pressure sometimes comes from their parents. Most parents are well (36)_____, but some of them aren't very helpful with the problems their sons and daughters have in (37)_____ to college, and a few of them seem to go out of their way to add to their children's difficulties.

For one thing, parents are often not (38)_____ of the kinds of problems their children face. They don't realize that the (39)_____ is keener, that the required (40)_____ of work are higher, and that their children may not be prepared for the change. (41)_____ to seeing A's and B's on high school report cards, they may be upset when their children's first (42)_____ college grades are below that level. At their kindest, they may gently (43)_____ why John or Mary isn't doing better, whether he or she is trying as hard as he or she should, and so on. (44)_____.

Sometimes parents regard their children as extensions of themselves and (45)_____. In their involvement and identification with their children, they forget that everyone is different and that each person must develop in his or her own way. They forget that their children, (46)_____.

Part IV Reading Comprehension
(*Reading in Depth*) (*25 minutes*)

Section A

Directions: *In this section, there is a passage with ten blanks. You are required to select one word for each blank from a list of choices given in a word bank following the passage. Read the passage through carefully before making your choices. Each choice in bank is identified by a letter. Please mark the corresponding letter for each item on **Answer Sheet 2** with a single line through the center.* ***You may not use any of the words in the bank more than once.***

Years ago, doctors often said that pain was a normal part of life. In particular, when older patients __47__ of pain, they were told it was a natural part of aging and they would have to learn to live with it.

Times have changed. Today, we take pain __48__. Indeed, pain is now considered the fifth vital sign, as important as blood pressure, temperature, breathing rate and pulse in __49__ a person's well-being. We know that *chronic* (慢性的) pain can *disrupt* (扰乱) a person's life, causing problems that __50__ from missed work to depression.

That's why a growing number of hospitals now depend upon physicians who __51__ in pain medicine. Not only do we evaluate the cause of the pain, which can help us treat the pain better, but we also help provide comprehensive therapy for depression and other psychological and social __52__ related to chronic pain. Such comprehensive therapy often __53__ the work of social workers, *psychiatrists* (心理医生) and psychologists, as well as specialists in pain medicine.

This modern __54__ for pain management has led to a wealth of innovative treatments which are more effective and with fewer side effects than ever before. Decades ago, there were only a __55__ number of drugs available, and many of them caused __56__ side effects in older people, including dizziness and fatigue. This created a double-edged sword: the medications helped relieve the pain but caused other problems that could be worse than the pain itself.

注意:此部分试题请在答题卡 2 上作答。

120

A. result	I. determining
B. involves	J. limited
C. significant	K. gravely
D. range	L. complained
E. relieved	M. respect
F. issues	N. prompting
G. seriously	O. specialize
H. magnificent	

Section B

Directions: *There are 2 passages in this section. Each passage is followed by some questions or unfinished statements. For each of them there are four choices marked A, B, C and D. You should decide on the best choice and mark the corresponding letter on **Answer Sheet 2** with a single line through the center.*

Passage One

Questions 57 to 61 are based on the following passage.

I've been writing for most of my life. The book *Writing Without Teachers* introduced me to one distinction and one practice that has helped my writing processes tremendously. The distinction is between the creative mind and the critical mind. While you need to employ both to get to a finished result, they cannot work in parallel no matter how much we might like to think so.

Trying to criticize writing on the fly is possibly the single greatest barrier to writing that most of us encounter. If you are listening to that 5th grade English teacher correct your grammar while you are trying to capture a *fleeting* (稍纵即逝的) thought, the thought will die. If you capture the fleeting thought and simply share it with the world in raw form, no one is likely to understand. You must learn to create first and then criticize if you want to make writing the tool for thinking that it is.

The practice that can help you past your learned bad habits of trying to edit as you write is what Elbow calls "free writing". In free writing, the objective is to get words down on paper non-stop, usually for 15 ~ 20 minutes. No stopping, no going back, no criticizing. The goal is to get the words flowing. As the words begin to flow, the ideas will come out from the shadows and let themselves be captured on your notepad or your screen.

Now you have raw materials that you can begin to work with using the critical mind that you've persuaded to sit on the side and watch quietly. Most likely, you will believe that this will take more time than you actually have and you will end up staring blankly at the page as the deadline draws near.

Instead of staring at a blank screen start filling it with words no matter how bad. Halfway

121

through your available time, stop and rework your raw writing into something closer to finished product. Move back and forth until you run out of time and the final result will most likely be far better than your current practices.

注意:此部分试题请在答题卡 2 上作答。

57. When the author says the creative mind and the critical mind "cannot work in parallel" (Line 4, Para. 1) in the writing process, he means _____ .

　　A. no one can be both creative and critical

　　B. they cannot be regarded as equally important

　　C. they are in constant conflict with each other

　　D. one cannot use them at the same time

58. What prevents people from writing on is _____ .

　　A. putting their ideas in raw form

　　B. attempting to edit as they write

　　C. ignoring grammatical soundness

　　D. trying to capture fleeting thoughts

59. What is the chief objective of the first stage of writing?

　　A. To organize one's thoughts logically.

　　B. To choose an appropriate topic.

　　C. To get one's ideas down.

　　D. To collect raw materials.

60. One common concern of writers about "free writing" is that _____ .

　　A. it overstresses the role of the creative mind

　　B. it takes too much time to edit afterwards

　　C. it may bring about too much criticism

　　D. it does not help them to think clearly

61. In what way does the critical mind help the writer in the writing process?

　　A. It refines his writing into better shape.

　　B. It helps him to come up with new ideas.

　　C. It saves the writing time available to him.

　　D. It allows him to sit on the side and observe.

Passage Two

Questions 62 to 66 are based on the following passage.

　　I don't ever want to talk about being a woman scientist again. There was a time in my life when people asked constantly for stories about what it's like to work in a field dominated by men. I was never very good at telling those stories because truthfully I never found them interesting. What I do find interesting is the origin of the universe, the shape of space-time and the nature of black holes.

At 19, when I began studying astrophysics, it did not bother me in the least to be the only woman in the classroom. But while earning my Ph.D. at MIT and then as a post-doctor doing space research, the issue started to bother me. My every achievement—jobs, research papers, awards—was viewed through the lens of *gender* (性别) politics. So were my failures. Sometimes, when I was pushed into an argument on left brain *versus* (相对于) right brain, or nature versus *nurture* (培育), I would instantly fight fiercely on my behalf and all woman-kind.

Then one day a few years ago, out of my mouth came a sentence that would eventually become my reply to any and all provocations: I don't talk about that anymore. It took me 10 years to get back the confidence I had at 19 and to realize that I didn't want to deal with gender issues. Why should curing sexism be yet another terrible burden on every female scientist? After all, I don't study sociology or political theory.

Today I research and teach at Barnard, a women's college in New York City. Recently, someone asked me how many of the 45 students in my class were women. You cannot imagine my satisfaction at being able to answer, 45. I know some of my students worry how they will manage their scientific research and a desire for children. And I don't dismiss those concerns. Still, I don't tell them "war" stories. Instead, I have given them this: the visual of their physics professor heavily pregnant doing physics experiments. And in turn they have given me the image of 45 women driven by a love of science. And that's a sight worth talking about.

注意：此部分试题请在答题卡 2 上作答。

62. Why doesn't the author want to talk about being a woman scientist again?

    A. She feels unhappy working in male-dominated fields.

    B. She is fed up with the issue of gender discrimination.

    C. She is not good at telling stories of the kind.

    D. She finds space research more important.

63. From Paragraph 2, we can infer that people would attribute the author's failures to _____.

    A. the very fact that she is a woman

    B. her involvement in gender politics

    C. her over-confidence as a female astrophysicist

    D. the burden she bears in a male-dominated society

64. What did the author constantly fight against while doing her Ph.D. and post-doctoral research?

    A. Lack of confidence in succeeding in space science.

    B. Unfair accusations from both inside and outside her circle.

C. People's stereotyped attitude towards female scientists.

D. Widespread misconceptions about nature and nurture.

65. Why does the author feel great satisfaction when talking about her class?

A. Female students no longer have to bother about gender issues.

B. Her students' performance has brought back her confidence.

C. Her female students can do just as well as male students.

D. More female students are pursuing science than before.

66. What does the image the author presents to her students suggest?

A. Women students needn't have the concerns of her generation.

B. Women have more barriers on their way to academic success.

C. Women can balance a career in science and having a family.

D. Women now have fewer problems pursuing a science career.

Part IV   Cloze (15 minutes)

Directions: *There are 20 blanks in the following passage. For each blank there are four choices marked A, B, C and D on the right side of the paper. You should choose the ONE that best fits into the passage. Then mark the corresponding letters on* **Answer Sheet 2** *with a single line through the center.*

注意：此部分试题请在答题卡 2 上作答。

An earthquake hit Kashmir on Oct. 8, 2005. It took some 75,000 lives, __67__ 130, 000 and left nearly 3.5 million without food, jobs or homes. __68__ overnight, scores of tent villages bloomed __69__ the region, tended by international aid organizations, military __70__ __ and aid groups working day and night to shelter the survivors before winter set __71__ .

Mercifully, the season was mild. But with the __72__ of spring, the refugees will be moved again. Camps that __73__ health care, food and shelter for 150,000 survivors have begun to close as they were __74__ intended to be permanent.

For most of the refugees, the thought of going back brings __75__ emotions. The past six months have been difficult. Families of __76__ many as 10 people have had to shelter __77__ a single tent and share cookstoves and bathing __78__ with neighbors. "They are looking forward to the clean water of their rivers", officials say. "They are __79__ of free fresh fruit. They want to get back to their herds and start __80__ again." But most will be returning to __ __81__ but heaps of ruins. In many villages, electrical __82__ have not been repaired, nor have roads. Aid workers __83__ that it will take years to rebuild what the earthquake took __84__ . And for the thousands of survivors, the __85__ will never be complete.

Yet the survivors have to start somewhere. New homes can be built __86__ the stones, bricks and beams of old ones. Spring is coming and it is a good time to start again.

67. A. injured   B. ruined   C. destroyed   D. damaged
68. A. Altogether   B. Almost   C. Scarcely   D. Surely
69. A. among   B. above   C. amid   D. across
70. A. ranks   B. equipment   C. personnel   D. installations
71. A. out   B. in   C. on   D. forth
72. A. falling   B. emergence   C. arrival   D. appearing
73. A. strengthened   B. aided   C. transferred   D. provided
74. A. never   B. once   C. ever   D. yet
75. A. puzzled   B. contrasted   C. doubled   D. mixed
76. A. like   B. as   C. so   D. too
77. A. by   B. below   C. under   D. with
78. A. facilities   B. instruments   C. implements   D. appliances
79. A. seeking   B. dreaming   C. longing   D. searching
80. A. producing   B. cultivating   C. farming   D. nourishing
81. A. anything   B. something   C. everything   D. nothing
82. A. lines   B. channels   C. paths   D. currents
83. A. account   B. measure   C. estimate   D. evaluate
84. A. aside   B. away   C. up   D. out
85. A. reservation   B. retreat   C. replacement   D. recovery
86. A. from   B. through   C. upon   D. onto

Part VI   Translation （5 minutes）

Directions: *Complete the sentences by translating into English the Chinese given in brackets.*
*Please write your translation on **Answer Sheet 2**.*

注意：此部分试题请在答题卡 2 上作答。

87. The finding of this study failed to _____ （将人们的睡眠质量考虑在内）.

88. The prevention and treatment of AIDS is _____ （我们可以合作的领域）.

89. Because of the leg injury, the athlete _____ （决定退出比赛）.

90. To make donations or for more information, please _____ （按以下地址和我们联系）.

91. Please come here at ten tomorrow morning _____ （如果你方便的话）.

2007 年 6 月 23 日大学英语
四级考试 A 卷参考答案
COLLEGE ENGLISH TEST (Band Four)

Part I Writing

参考范文

Welcome to our clubs!

Welcome to join the English club! Do you have questions on how to overcome the difficulties in English learning? Do you want to know how to pass the College English Test? Do you want to improve your oral English? You will find out the answers from our activities.

The activities in English club will help you to improve your oral English which can give you an advantage in job interview. As the proverb goes, practice makes perfect. We provide you the opportunity to practice your oral English. Some people complain of the minimum chance to open their mouth to speak. The chance is right in front of you, so why hesitate?

If you want to join us, just call us at 02088888888 or send an E-mail to englishclub @ cet. edu. cn, with personal information attached. And after two days, you will be a member of our club. So don't hesitate, join us!

Part II Reading Comprehension (Skimming and Scanning)

1. Y 2. Y 3. N 4. Y 5. NG 6. N 7. Y

8. unwelcome E-mails   9. names and contact information   10. economic gain

Part III Listening Comprehension

Section A

11. C. It might appeal more to viewers over 40.

12. D. The man admires the woman's talent in writing.

13. B. The woman saved the man some trouble.

14. A. He quit teaching in June.

15. C. She only read part of the book.

16. D. She had been away from school to attend to her husband.

17. D. The Smith's new house is not far from their old one.

18. A. The man had a hard time finding a parking place.

19. C. The hotel clerk tried to take advantage of his inexperience.

20. B. There was a conference going on in the city.

21.A. It was free of charge on weekends.

22.C. Complain to the hotel manager.

23.B. Assistant Director of the Admission Office.

24.A. Nearly fifty percent are foreigners.

25.C. She will be more involved in policy making.

Section B

26.C. Her parents immigrated to America.

27.B. He was crippled in a car accident.

28.D. She was highly devoted to her family.

29.C. He was seriously injured.

30.A. He was able to talk again.

31.B. Two and a half months.

32.D. They declined to give details of his condition.

33.A. For people to share ideas and show farm products.

34.B. By bring a bag of grain in exchange for a ticket.

35.D. They remind the Americans of the importance of agriculture.

Section C

36. meaning   37. adjusting   38. aware   39. competition   40. standards

41. accustomed   42. semester   43. inquire

44. At their worst, they may threaten to take their children out of college or cut off bunds

45. think it only right and natural that they determine what their children do with their lives

46. who are now young adults must be the ones responsible for what they do and what they are

Part IV   Reading Comprehension (Reading in Depth)

Section A

47.L. complained   48.G. seriously   49.I. determining   50.D. range   51.O. specialize

52.F. issues   53.B. involves   54.M. respect   55.J. limited 56.C. significant

Section B

57.D. one cannot use them at the same time

58.B. attempting to edit as they write

59.C. To get one's ideas down.

60.B. it takes too much time to edit afterwards

61.A. It refines his writing into better shape.

62.B. She is fed up with the issue of gender discrimination.

63.A. the very fact that she is a woman

64.C. People's stereotyped attitude towards female scientists.

65.D. More female students are pursuing science than before.

66. C. Women can balance a career in science and having a family.

Part V Cloze

67. A. injured	68. B. Almost	69. D. across	70. C. personnel	71. B. in
72. C. arrival	73. D. provided	74. A. never	75. D. mixed	76. B. as
77. C. under	78. A. facilities	79. B. dreaming	80. C. farming	81. D. nothing
82. A. lines	83. C. estimate	84. B. away	85. D. recovery	86. A. from

Part VI Translation

87. take people's sleep quality into account

88. the field (where) we can cooperate / the field in which we can cooperate

89. decided to quit the match

90. contact us at the following address

91. if it is convenient for you / at your convenience

2007 年 6 月 23 日大学英语
四级考试 A 卷听力原文
COLLEGE ENGLISH TEST(Band Four)

Part III Listening Comprehension

Section A

11. W: Did you watch the 7 o'clock program on Channel 2 yesterday evening? I was about to watch it when someone came to see me.

    M: Yeah. It reported some major breakthroughs in cancer research. People over 40 would find the program worth watching.

    Q: What do we learn from the conversation about the TV program?

12. W: I won the first prize in the national writing contest and I got this camera as an award.

    M: It's a good camera. You can take it when you travel. I had no idea you were a marvelous writer.

    Q: What do we learn from the conversation?

13. M: I wish I hadn't thrown away that waiting list.

    W: I thought you might regret it. That's why I picked it up from the waste paper basket and left it on the desk.

    Q: What do we learn from the conversation?

14. W: Are you still teaching at the junior high school?

    M: Not since June. My brother and I opened a restaurant as soon as he got out of the army.

    Q: What do we learn about the man from the conversation?

15. M: Hi, Susan. Have you finished reading the book Prof. Johnson recommended?

W: Oh, I haven't read it through the way I'd read a novel. I just read a few chapters which interested me.

Q: What does the woman mean?

16. M: Jane missed class again, didn't she? I wonder why.

W: Well, I knew she had been absent all week, so I called her this morning to see if she was sick. It turned out that her husband was badly injured in a car accident.

Q: What does the woman say about Jane?

17. W: I'm sure that Smith's new house is somewhere on this street, but I don't know exactly where it is.

M: But I'm told it's two blocks from their old home.

Q: What do we learn from the conversation?

18. W: I've been waiting here almost half an hour. How come it took it so long?

M: Sorry, honey. I had to drive two blocks before I spotted a place to park the car.

Q: What do we learn from the conversation?

Conversation One

M: Hello, I have a reservation for tonight.

W: Your name, please?

M: Nelson, Charles Nelson.

W: OK, Mr. Nelson, that's a room for 5 and ...

M: Excuse me? You mean a room for 5 pounds? I didn't know the special was so good.

W: No, no, no, according to our records, a room for 5 guests was booked under your name.

M: No, no, hold on. You must have two guests under the name.

W: OK, let me check this again. Oh, here we are.

M: Yes?

W: Charles Nelson, a room for one for the nineteen...

M: Wait, wait, it was for tonight, not tomorrow night.

W: Ehm, hmm, I don't think we have any rooms for tonight. There is a conference going on in town and, er, let's see, yeah, no rooms.

M: Oh, come on, you must have something, anything!

W: Well, let, let me check my computer here. Ah!

M: What?

W: There has been a cancellation for this evening. A honeymoon suite is now available.

M: Great, I'll take it.

W: But I'll have to charge you a hundred and fifty pounds for the night.

M: What? I should get a discount for the inconvenience!

W: Well, the best I can give you is a 10% discount, plus a ticket for a free continental breakfast.

M: Hey, isn't the breakfast free anyway?

W: Well, only on weekends.

M: I want to talk to the manager.

W: Wait, wait, wait, Mr. Nelson, I think I can give you an additional 15% discount!

Questions 19 to 22 are based on the conversation you have just heard.

19. What is the man's problem?

20. Why did the hotel clerk say they didn't have any rooms for that night?

21. What did the clerk say about the breakfast in the hotel?

22. What did the man imply he would do at the end of the conversation?

Conversation Two

M: Sarah, you work in the admission's office, don't you?

W: Yes, I'm, I've been here 10 years as an assistance director.

M: Really? What does that involve?

W: Well, I'm in charge of all the admissions of post graduate students in the university.

M: Only post graduates?

W: Yes, post graduates only. I have nothing at all to do with undergraduates.

M: Do you find that you get a particular... sort of different national groups? I mean you get larger numbers from Latin America or...

W: Yes, well, of all the students enrolled last year, nearly half were from overseas. They were from the Afican countries, the far east, the middle east and Latin America.

M: Ehm, but have you been doing just that for the last 10 years or have you done other things?

W: Well, I've been doing the same job, ehm, before that I was a secretary of the medical school at Birmingham, and further back I worked in the local government.

M: Oh, I see.

W: So I've done different types of things.

M: Yes, indeed. How do you imagine your job might develop in the future? Can you imagine shifting into a different kind of responsibility or doing something...?

W: Oh, yeah, from October 1st I'll be doing an entirely different job. There is going to be more committee work. I mean, more policy work, and less dealing with students unfortunately. I'll miss my contact with students.

Questions 23 to 25 are based on the conversation you have just heard.

23. What is the woman's present position?

24. What do we learn about the post graduates enrolled last year in the woman's university?

25. What will the woman's new job be like?

130

Section B

Passage One

My mother was born in a small town in northern Italy. She was three when her parents immigrated to America in 1926. They lived in Chicago, where my grandfather worked making ice-cream. Mama thrived in the urban environment. At 16, she graduated first in her high school class, went on to secretarial school and finally worked as an executive secretary for a rare wood company. She was beautiful too. When a local photographer used her pictures in his monthly window display, she felt pleased. Her favorite portrait showed her sitting by Lake Michigan, her hair wind-blown, her gaze reaching towards the horizon.

My parents were married in 1944. Dad was a quiet and intelligent man. He was 17 when he left Italy. Soon after, a hit-and-run accident left him with a permanent limp. Dad worked hard selling candy to Chicago office workers on their break. He had little formal schooling. His English was self-taught. Yet he eventually built a small successful whole-sale candy business. Dad was generous and handsome. Mama was devoted to him. After she married, my mother quit her job and gave herself to her family.

In 1950, with three small children, Dad moved the family to a farm 40 miles from Chicago. He worked the land and commuted to the city to run his business. Mama said good-bye to her parents and friends and traded her busy city neighborhood for a more isolated life. But she never complained.

Questions 26 to 28 are based on the passage you have just heard.

26. What does the speaker tell us about his mother's early childhood?
27. What do we learn about the speaker's father?
28. What does the speaker say about his mother?

Passage Two

During a 1995 roof collapse, a fire fighter named Donald Herbert was left brain damaged. For 10 years he was unable to speak. Then one Saturday morning, he did something that shocked his family and doctors — he started speaking. "I want to talk to my wife," Donald Herbert said out of the blue. Staff members of the nursing home where he has lived for more than 7 years rose to get Linda Herbert on the telephone. "It was the first of many conversations the 44-year-old patient had with his family and friends during the 14 hour stretch." Herbert's uncle Simon Manka said. "How long have I been away?" Herbert asked. "We told him almost 10 years." The uncle said. He thought it was only three months.

Herbert was fighting a house fire Dec. 29, 1995, when the roof collapsed burying him underneath. After going without air for several minutes, Herbert was unconscious for two and a half months and has undergone therapy ever since.

News accounts in the days and years after his injury, described Herbert as blind and with

131

little, if any, memory. A video shows him receiving physical therapy, but apparently unable to communicate and with little awareness of his surroundings. Manka declined to discuss his nephew's current condition or whether the apparent progress was continuing. "The family was seeking privacy while doctors evaluated Herbert," he said. As word of Herbert's progress spread, visitors streamed into the nursing home. "He is resting comfortably," the uncle told them.

Questions 29 to 32 are based on the passage you have just heard.

29. What happened to Herbert 10 years ago?

30. What surprised Donald Herbert's family and doctors one Saturday?

31. How long did Herbert remain unconscious?

32. How did Herbert's family react to the public attention?

Passage Three

Almost all states in America have a state fair. They last for one, two or three weeks. The Indiana state fair is one of the largest and oldest state fairs in the United States. It is held every summer.

It started in 1852. Its goals were to educate, share ideas and present Indiana's best products. The cost of a single ticket to enter the fair was 20 cents. During the early 1930's, officials of the fair ruled that people could attend by paying something other than money. For example, farmers brought a bag of grain in exchange for a ticket.

With the passage of time, the fair has grown and changed a lot. But it is still one of the Indiana's celebrated events. People from all over Indiana and from many other states attend the fair.

They can do many things at the fair. They can watch the judging of the priced cows, pigs and other animals. They can see sheep getting their wool cut and they can learn how that wool is made into clothing. They can watch cows giving birth. In fact, people can learn about animals they would never see except other fair. The fair provides the chance for the farming community to show its skills and fun products. For example, visitors might see the world's largest apple or the tallest sun flower plant.

Today, children and adults at the fair can play new computer games or attempt more traditional games of skill. They can watch performances put on by famous entertainers. Experts say such fairs are important because people need to remember that they are connected to the earth and its products and they depend on animals for many things.

Questions 33 to 35 are based on the passage you have just heard.

33. What were the main goals of the Indiana state fair when it started?

34. How did some farmers give entrance to the fair in the early 1930's?

35. Why are state fairs important events in the America?

Section C

Students' pressure sometimes comes from their parents. Most parents are well-meaning, but some of them aren't very helpful with the problems their sons and daughters have in adjusting to college. And a few of them seem to go out of their way to add to their children's difficulties. For one thing, parents are often not aware of the kinds of problems their children face. They don't realize that the competition is keener, that the required standards of work are higher, and that their children may not be prepared for the change. Accustomed to seeing A's and B's on high school report cards, they may be upset when their children's first semester college grades are below that level. At their kindest, they may gently enquire why John or Mary isn't doing better, whether he or she is trying as hard as he or she should, and so on. At their worst, they may threaten to take their children out of college or cut off funds. Sometimes parents regard their children as extensions of themselves and think it only right and natural that they determine what their children do with their lives. In their involvement and identification with their children, they forget that everyone is different and that each person must develop in his or her own way. They forget that their children, who are now young adults, must be the ones responsible for what they do and what they are.

2007 年 12 月 22 日大学英语四级考试 B 卷
COLLEGE ENGLISH TEST
– Band Four –

Part I   Writing（30 minutes）

Directions：
1.各大学开设了各种各样的选修课；
2.学生因为各种原因选择了不同的选修课；
3.以你自己为例。

Part II   Reading Comprehension
（Skimming and Scanning）（15 minutes）

Directions：*In this part，you will have 15 minutes to go over the passage quickly and answer the questions on **Answer Sheet 1**. For questions 1 ~ 7，choose the best answer from the four choices marked A，B，C and D. For questions 8 ~ 10，complete the sentences with the information given in the passage.*

Universities Branch Out

As never before in their long history，universities have become instruments of national competition as well as instruments of peace. They are the place of the scientific discoveries that move economies forward，and the primary means of educating the talent required to obtain and maintain competitive advantage. But at the same time，the opening of national borders to the flow of goods，services，information and especially people has made universities a powerful force for global integration，mutual understanding and geopolitical stability.

In response to the same forces that have driven the world economy，universities have become more self-consciously global：seeking students from around the world who represent the entire range of cultures and values，sending their own students abroad to prepare them for global careers，offering courses of study that address the challenges of an interconnected world and *collaborative*（合作的）research programs to advance science for the benefit of all humanity.

Of the forces shaping higher education none is more sweeping than the movement across borders. Over the past three decades the number of students leaving home each year to study abroad has grown at an annual rate of 3.9 percent, from 800,000 in 1975 to 2.5 million in 2004. Most travel from one developed nation to another, but the flow from developing to developed countries is growing rapidly. The reverse flow, from developed to developing countries, is on the rise, too. Today foreign students earn 30 percent of the doctoral degrees awarded in the United States and 38 percent of those in the United Kingdom. And the number crossing borders for undergraduate study is growing as well, to 8 percent of the undergraduates at America's best institutions and 10 percent of all undergraduates in the U.K. In the United States, 20 percent of the newly hired professors in science and engineering are foreign-born, and in China many newly hired faculty members at the top research universities received their graduate education abroad.

Universities are also encouraging students to spend some of their undergraduate years in another country. In Europe, more than 140,000 students participate in the Erasmus program each year, taking courses for credit in one of 2,200 participating institutions across the continent. And in the United States, institutions are helping place students in the summer *internships* (实习) abroad to prepare them for global careers. Yale and Harvard have led the way, offering every undergraduate at least one international study or internship opportunity—and providing the financial resources to make it possible.

Globalization is also reshaping the way research is done. One new trend involves sourcing portions of a research program to another country. Yale professor and Howard Hughes Medical Institute investigator Tian Xu directs a research center focused on the genetics of human disease at Shanghai's Fudan University, in collaboration with faculty colleagues from both schools. The Shanghai center has 95 employees and graduate students working in a 4,300-square-meter laboratory facility. Yale faculty, post-doctors and graduate students visit regularly and attend videoconference seminars with scientists from both campuses. The arrangement benefits both countries; Xu's Yale lab is more productive, thanks to the lower costs of conducting research in China, and Chinese graduate students, post doctors and faculty get on-the-job training from a world-class scientist and his U.S. team.

As a result of its strength in science, the United States has consistently led the world in the commercialization of major new technologies, from the mainframe computer and the integrated circuit of the 1960s to the Internet *infrastructure* (基础设施) and applications software of the 1990s. The link between university-based science and industrial application is often indirect but sometimes highly visible: Silicon Valley was intentionally created by Stanford University, and Route 128 outside Boston has long housed companies spun off from MIT and Harvard. Around the world, governments have encouraged copying of this model, perhaps most successfully in Cambridge, England, where Microsoft and scores of other leading software and biotechnology companies have set up shop around the university.

For all its success, the United States remains deeply hesitant about sustaining the research-university model. Most politicians recognize the link between investment in science and national economic strength, but support for research funding has been unsteady. The budget of the National Institutes of Health doubled between 1998 and 2003, but has risen more slowly than inflation since then. Support for the physical sciences and engineering barely kept pace with inflation during that same period. The attempt to make up lost ground is welcome, but the nation would be better served by steady, predictable increases in science funding at the rate of long-term GDP growth, which is on the order of inflation plus 3 percent per year.

American politicians have great difficulty recognizing that admitting more foreign students can greatly promote the national interest by increasing international understanding. Adjusted for inflation, public funding for international exchanges and foreign-language study is well below the levels of 40 years ago. In the wake of September 11, changes in the visa process caused a dramatic decline in the number of foreign students seeking admission to U.S. universities, and a corresponding surge in enrollments in Australia, Singapore and the U.K. Objections from American university and business leaders led to improvements in the process and a reversal of the decline, but the United States is still seen by many as unwelcoming to international students.

Most Americans recognize that universities contribute to the nation's well-being through their scientific research, but many fear that foreign students threaten American competitiveness by taking their knowledge and skills back home. They fail to grasp that welcoming foreign students to the United States has two important positive effects: first, the very best of them stay in the States and—like immigrants throughout history—strengthen the nation; and second, foreign students who study in the United States become ambassadors for many of its most *cherished* (珍视) values when they return home. Or at least they understand them better. In America as elsewhere, few instruments of foreign policy are as effective in promoting peace and stability as welcoming international university students.

注意:此部分试题请在答题卡 1 上作答。

1. From the first paragraph we know that present-day universities have become _____ .

  A. more popularized than ever before   B. in-service training organizations

  C. a powerful force for global integration   D. more and more research-oriented

2. Over the past three decades, the enrollment of overseas students has increased _____ .

  A. at an annual rate of 8 percent   B. at an annual rate of 3.9 percent

  C. by 800,000   D. by 2.5 million

3. In the United States, how many of the newly hired professors in science and engineering are

foreign-born?

    A. 38%.   B. 10%.   C. 30%.   D. 20%.

4. How do Yale and Harvard prepare their undergraduates for global careers?

    A. They give them chances for international study or internship.

    B. They arrange for them to participate in the Erasmus program.

    C. They offer them various courses in international politics.

    D. They organize a series of seminars on world economy.

5. An example illustrating the general trend of universities' globalization is _____.

    A. Yale's establishing branch campuses throughout the world

    B. Yale's student exchange program with European institutions

    C. Yale's helping Chinese universities to launch research projects

    D. Yale's collaboration with Fudan University on genetic research

6. What do we learn about Silicon Valley from the passage?

    A. It is known to be the birthplace of Microsoft Company.

    B. It was intentionally created by Stanford University.

    C. It is where the Internet infrastructure was built up.

    D. It houses many companies spun off from MIT and Harvard.

7. What is said about the U.S. federal funding for research?

    A. It has increased by 3 percent.   B. It doubled between 1998 and 2003.

    C. It has been unsteady for years.   D. It has been more than sufficient.

8. The dramatic decline in the enrollment of foreign students in the U.S. after September 11 was caused by _____.

9. Many Americans fear that American competitiveness may be threatened by foreign students who will _____.

10. The policy of welcoming foreign students can benefit the U.S. in that the very best of them will stay and _____.

Part III Listening Comprehension (35 minutes)

Section A

Directions: *In this section, you will hear 8 short conversations and 2 long conversations. At the end of each conversation, one or more questions will be asked about what was said. Both the conversation and the questions will be spoken only once. After each question there will be a pause. During the pause, you must read the four choices marked A, B, C and D, and decide which is the best answer. Then marked the corresponding letter on* **Answer Sheet 2** *with a single line through the centre.*

11. A. She used to be in poor health.   B. She didn't do well at high school.

    C. She was popular among boys.   D. She was somewhat overweight.

12. A. At the airport.   B. At the hotel reception.

    C. In a restaurant.   D. In a booking office.

13. A. Having confidence in her son.   B. Telling her son not to worry.

    C. Teaching her son by herself.   D. Asking the teacher for extra help.

14. A. Have a short break.   B. Take two weeks off.

    C. Go on vacation with the man.   D. Continue her work outdoors.

15. A. He is taking care of his twin brother.   B. He is worried about Rod's health.

    C. He has been in perfect condition.   D. He has been feeling ill all week.

16. A. She bought a new set of furniture from Italy last month.

    B. She sold all her furniture before she moved house.

    C. She plans to put all her old furniture in the basement.

    D. She still keeps some old furniture in her new house.

17. A. The woman forgot lending the book to the man.

    B. The woman doesn't find the book useful any more.

    C. The woman doesn't seem to know what the book is about.

    D. The woman wondered why the man didn't return the book.

18. A. Most of the man's friends are athletes.

    B. The man doesn't look like a sportsman.

    C. Few people share the woman's opinion.

    D. The woman doubts the man's athletic ability.

Questions 19 to 22 are based on the conversation you have just heard.

19. A. She is afraid that she has lost it.   B. She is going to get it at the airport.

    C. She has packed it in one of her bags.   D. She has probably left it in a taxi.

20. A. It will cost her a lot.   B. It will last one week.

    C. It ends in winter.   D. It depends on the weather.

21. A. There is a lot of stuff to pack.   B. There might be a traffic jam.

    C. The plane is taking off soon.   D. The taxi is waiting for them.

22. A. At home.   B. In the man's car.

    C. By the side of a taxi.   D. At the airport.

Questions 23 to 25 are based on the conversation you have just heard.

23. A. She is thirsty for promotion.   B. She is tired of her present work.

    C. She wants a much higher salary.   D. She wants to save travel expenses.

24. A. Language instructor.   B. Environmental engineer.

C. Translator.   D. Travel agent.

25. A. Devotion and work efficiency.   B. Lively personality and inquiring mind.

    C. Communication skills and team spirit.   D. Education and experience.

Section B

Directions: *In this section, you will hear 3 short passages. At the end of each passage, you will hear some questions. Both the passage and the questions will be spoken only once. After you hear a question, you must choose the best answer from the four choices marked A, B, C and D. Then mark the corresponding letter on **Answer Sheet 2** with a single line through the center.*

注意:此部分试题请在答题卡 2 上作答。

Passage One

Questions 26 to 29 are based on the passage you have just heard.

26. A. They want children to keep them company.

    B. They want to enrich their life experience.

    C. They need looking after in their old age.

    D. They care a lot about children.

27. A. Their birth parents often try to conceal their birth information.

    B. They are usually adopted from distant places.

    C. Their birth information is usually kept secret.

    D. Their adoptive parents don't want them to know their birth parents.

28. A. They do not want to hurt the feelings of their adoptive parents.

    B. They have mixed feelings about finding their natural parents.

    C. They generally hold bad feelings towards their birth parents.

    D. They are fully aware of the expenses involved in the search.

29. A. Adoption has much to do with love.

    B. Understanding is the key to successful adoption.

    C. Most people prefer to adopt children from overseas.

    D. Early adoption makes for closer parent-child relationship.

Passage Two

Questions 30 to 32 are based on the passage you have just heard.

30. A. He suffered from mental illness.

    B. He bought *The Washington Post*.

    C. He was once a reporter for a major newspaper.

    D. He turned a failing newspaper into a success.

31. A. She committed suicide because of her mental disorder.

    B. She got her first job as a teacher at the University of Chicago.

    C. She was the first woman to lead a big U.S. publishing company.

D. She took over her father's position when he died.

32. A. Katharine had exerted an important influence on the world.

B. People came to see the role of women in the business world.

C. American media would be quite different without Katharine.

D. Katharine played a major part in reshaping Americans' mind.

Passage Three

Questions 33 to 35 are based on the passage you have just heard.

33. A. It'll allow them to receive free medical treatment.

B. It'll prevent the doctors from overcharging them.

C. It'll enable them to enjoy the best medical care.

D. It'll protect them from possible financial crises.

34. A. They may not be able to receive timely medical treatment.

B. They can only visit doctors who speak their native languages.

C. They have to go through very complicated application procedures.

D. They can't immediately get back the money paid for their medical cost.

35. A. They must send the receipts to the insurance company promptly.

B. They have to pay a much higher price to get an insurance policy.

C. They needn't pay the entire medical bill at once.

D. They don't have to pay for the medical services.

Section C

Directions: *In this section, you will hear a passage three times. When the passage is read for the first time, you should listen carefully for its general idea. When the passage is read for the second time, you are required to fill in the blanks numbered from 36 to 43 with the exact words you have just heard. For blanks numbered 44 to 46 you are required to fill in the missing information. For these blanks, you can either use the exact words you have just heard or write down the main points in your own words. Finally when the passage is read for the third time, you should check what you have written.*

注意:此部分试题请在答题卡 2 上作答。

More and more of the world's population are living in towns or cities. The speed at which cities are growing in the less developed countries is (36) _____ . Between 1920 and 1960 big cities in developed countries (37) _____ two and a half times in size, but in other parts of the world the growth was eight times their size.

The (38) _____ size of growth is bad enough, but there are now also very (39) _____ signs of trouble in the (40) _____ of percentages of people living in towns and percentages of people working in industry. During the nineteenth century cities grew as a result of the growth of industry. In Europe the (41) _____ of people living in cities was

140

always smaller than that of the (42) _____ working in factories. Now, however, the (43) _____ is almost always true in the newly industrialized world: (44)_____

_____ .

Without a base of people working in industry, these cities cannot pay for their growth; (45) _____ . There has been little opportunity to build water supplies or other facilities. (46)_____

_____ , a growth in the number of hopeless and despairing parents and starving children.

Part IV Reading Comprehension (*Reading in Depth*) (*25 minutes*)

Section A

Directions: *In this section, there is a passage with ten blanks. You are required to select one word for each blank from a list of choices given in a word bank following the passage. Read the passage through carefully before making your choices. Each choice in bank is identified by a letter. Please mark the corresponding letter for each item on **Answer Sheet 2** with a single line through the center. **You may not use any of the words in the bank more than once**.*

Questions 47 to 56 are based on the following passage.

As war spreads to many corners of the globe, children sadly have been drawn into the center of conflicts. In Afghanistan, Bosnia, and Colombia, however, groups of children have been taking part in peace education __47__ . The children, after learning to resolve conflicts, took on the __48__ of peacemakers. The Children's Movement for Peace in Colombia was even *nominated* (提名) for the Nobel Peace Prize in 1998. Groups of children __49__ as peacemakers studied human rights and poverty issues in Colombia, eventually forming a group with five other schools in Bogota known as The Schools of Peace.

The classroom __50__ opportunities for children to replace angry, violent behaviors with __51__ , peaceful ones. It is in the classroom that caring and respect for each person empowers children to take a step __52__ toward becoming peacemakers. Fortunately, educators have access to many online resources that are __53__ useful when helping children along the path to peace. The Young Peacemakers Club, started in 1992, provides a Website with resources for teachers and __54__ on starting a Kindness Campaign. The World Centers of Compassion for Children International call attention to children's rights and how to help the __55__ of war. Starting a Peacemakers' Club is a praiseworthy venture for a class and one that could spread to other classrooms and ideally affect the culture of the __56__ school.

注意:此部分试题请在答题卡 2 上作答。

A. victims	I. forward
B. technology	J. especially
C. role	K. entire
D. respectively	L. cooperative
E. projects	M. comprehensive
F. offers	N. assuming
G. information	O. acting
H. images	

Section B

Directions: *There are 2 passages in this section. Each passage is followed by some questions or unfinished statements. For each of them there are four choices marked A, B, C and D. You should decide on the best choice and mark the corresponding letter on **Answer Sheet 2** with a single line through the center.*

Passage One

Questions 57 to 61 are based on the following passage.

In this age of Internet chat, videogames and reality television, there is no shortage of mindless activities to keep a child occupied. Yet, despite the competition, my 8-year-old daughter Rebecca wants to spend her leisure time writing short stories. She wants to enter one of her stories into a writing contest, a competition she won last year.

As a writer I know about winning contests, and about losing them. I know what it is like to work hard on a story only to receive a rejection slip from the publisher. I also know the pressures of trying to live up to a reputation created by previous victories. What if she doesn't win the contest again? That's the strange thing about being a parent. So many of our own past scars and dashed hopes can surface.

A *revelation* (启示) came last week when I asked her, "Don't you want to win again?" "No," she replied, "I just want to tell the story of an angel going to first grade."

I had just spent weeks correcting her stories as she *spontaneously* (自发地) told them. Telling myself that I was merely an experienced writer guiding the young writer across the hall, I offered suggestions for characters, conflicts and endings for her tales. The story about a fearful angel starting first grade was quickly "guided" by me into the tale of a little girl with a wild imagination taking her first music lesson. I had turned her contest into my contest without even realizing it.

Staying back and giving kids space to grow is not as easy as it looks. Because I know very little about farm animals who use tools or angels who go to first grade, I had to accept the fact that I was *co-opting* (借用) my daughter's experience.

While stepping back was difficult for me, it was certainly a good first step that I will

142

quickly follow with more steps, putting myself far enough away to give her room but close enough to help if asked. All the while I will be reminding myself that children need room to experiment, grow and find their own voices.

注意：此部分试题请在答题卡 2 上作答。

57. What do we learn from the first paragraph?

   A. A lot of distractions compete for children's time nowadays.

   B. Children do find lots of fun in many mindless activities.

   C. Rebecca is much too occupied to enjoy her leisure time.

   D. Rebecca draws on a lot of online materials for her writing.

58. What did the author say about her own writing experience?

   A. She was constantly under pressure of writing more.

   B. Most of her stories had been rejected by publishers.

   C. She did not quite live up to her reputation as a writer.

   D. Her way to success was full of pains and frustrations.

59. Why did Rebecca want to enter this year's writing contest?

   A. She had won a prize in the previous contest.

   B. She wanted to share her stories with readers.

   C. She was sure of winning with her mother's help.

   D. She believed she possessed real talent for writing.

60. The author took great pains to refine her daughter's stories because _____.

   A. she wanted to help Rebecca realize her dream of becoming a writer

   B. she was afraid Rebecca's imagination might run wild while writing

   C. she did not want to disappoint Rebecca who needed her help so much

   D. she believed she had the knowledge and experience to offer guidance

61. What's the author's advice for parents?

   A. Children should be given every chance to voice their opinions.

   B. Parents should keep an eye on the activities their kids engage in.

   C. Children should be allowed freedom to grow through experience.

   D. A writing career, though attractive, is not for every child to pursue.

Passage Two

Questions 62 to 66 are based on the following passage.

By almost any measure, there is a boom in Internet-based instruction. In just a few years, 34 percent of American universities have begun offering some form of distance learning (DL), and among the larger schools, it's closer to 90 percent. If you doubt the popularity of the trend, you probably haven't heard of the University of Phoenix. It grants degrees entirely on the basis of online instruction. It enrolls 90,000 students, a statistic used to support its claim to be the largest private university in the country.

While the kinds of instruction offered in these programs will differ, DL usually signifies a course in which the instructors post *syllabi* (课程大纲), reading assignments, and schedules on Websites, and students send in their assignments by E-mail. Generally speaking, face-to-face communication with an instructor is minimized or eliminated altogether.

The attraction for students might at first seem obvious. Primarily, there's the convenience promised by courses on the Net: you can do the work, as they say, in your *pajamas* (睡衣). But figures indicate that the reduced effort results in a reduced commitment to the course. While dropout rates for all freshmen at American universities is around 20 percent, the rate for online students is 35 percent. Students themselves seem to understand the weaknesses inherent in the setup. In a survey conducted for eCornell, the DL division of Cornell University, less than a third of the respondents expected the quality of the online course to be as good as the classroom course.

Clearly, from the schools' perspective, there's a lot of money to be saved. Although some of the more ambitious programs require new investments in servers and networks to support collaborative software, most DL courses can run on existing or minimally *upgraded* (升级) systems. The more students who enroll in a course but don't come to campus, the more the school saves on keeping the lights on in the classrooms, paying doorkeepers, and maintaining parking lots. And, while there's evidence that instructors must work harder to run a DL course for a variety of reasons, they won't be paid any more, and might well be paid less.

注意：此部分试题请在答题卡 2 上作答。

62. What is the most striking feature of the University of Phoenix?

A. It boasts the largest number of students on campus.

B. All its courses are offered onineline.

C. Its online courses are of the best quality.

D. Anyone taking its online courses is sure to get a degree.

63. According to the passage, distance learning is basically characterized by _____ .

A. a minimum or total absence of face-to-face instruction

B. a considerable flexibility in its academic requirements

C. the great diversity of students' academic backgrounds

D. the casual relationship between students and professors

64. Many students take Internet-based courses mainly because they can _____ .

A. save a great deal on traveling and boarding expenses

B. select courses from various colleges and universities

C. work on the required courses whenever and wherever

D. earn their academic degrees with much less effort

65. What accounts for the high drop-out rates for online students?

    A. There is no mechanism to ensure that they make the required effort.

    B. There is no strict control over the academic standards of the courses.

    C. The evaluation system used by online universities is inherently weak.

    D. Lack of classroom interaction reduces the effectiveness of instruction.

66. According to the passage, universities show great enthusiasm for DL programs for the purpose of _____ .

    A. building up their reputation   B. upgrading their teaching facilities

    C. providing convenience for students   D. cutting down on their expenses

Part V   Cloze (*15 minutes*)

Directions: *There are 20 blanks in the following passage. For each blank there are four choices marked A, B, C and D on the right side of the paper. You should choose the ONE that best fits into the passage. Then mark the corresponding letters on **Answer Sheet 2** with a single line through the center.*

注意：此部分试题请在答题卡 2 上作答。

    One factor that can influence consumers is their mood state. Mood may be defined __67__ a temporary and mild positive or negative feeling that is generalized and not tied __68__ any particular circumstance. Moods should be __69__ from emotions which are usually more intense, __70__ to specific circumstances, and often conscious. __71__ one sense, the effect of a consumer's mood can be thought of in __72__ the same way as can our reactions to the __73__ of our friends—when our friends are happy and "up", that tends to influence us positively __74__ when they are "down", that can have a __75__ impact on us. Similarly, consumers operating under a __76__ mood state tend to react to *stimuli* (刺激因素) in a direction __77__ with that mood state. Thus, for example, we should expect to see __78__ in a positive mood state evaluate products in more of a __79__ manner than they would when not in such a state. __80__, mood states appear capable of __81__ a consumer's memory.

    Moods appear to be __82__ influenced by marketing techniques. For example, the rhythm, pitch, and __83__ of music has been shown to influence behavior such as the __84__ of time spent in supermarkets or __85__ to purchase products. In addition, advertising can influence consumers' moods which, in __86__, are capable of influencing consumers' reactions to products.

67. A. with   B. about   C. as   D. by

68. A. up   B. to   C. under   D. over

69. A. divided   B. derived   C. descended   D. distinguished

70. A. referred	B. related	C. attached	D. associated
71. A. In	B. On	C. By	D. Of
72. A. thus	B. still	C. much	D. even
73. A. behavior	B. gesture	C. signal	D. view
74. A. for	B. provided	C. unless	D. but
75. A. relative	B. negative	C. sensitive	D. decisive
76. A. fixed	B. granted	C. given	D. driven
77. A. insistent	B. resistant	C. persistent	D. consistent
78. A. retailers	B. consumers	C. businessmen	D. manufacturers
79. A. casual	B. serious	C. favorable	D. critical
80. A. Moreover	B. However	C. Nevertheless	D. Otherwise
81. A. lifting	B. raising	C. cultivating	D. enhancing
82. A. rarely	B. readily	C. currently	D. cautiously
83. A. volume	B. speed	C. step	D. band
84. A. extent	B. scope	C. amount	D. range
85. A. capacities	B. facilities	C. intentions	D. reflections
86. A. turn	B. depth	C. total	D. detail

Part VI Translation（*5 minutes*）

Directions: *Complete the sentences by translating into English the Chinese given in brackets.*
*Please write your translation on **Answer Sheet 2***

注意：此部分试题请在答题卡 **2** 上作答。

87. _____（多亏了一系列的新发明），doctors can treat this disease successfully.

88. In my sixties, one change I notice is that _____（我比以前更容易累了）.

89. I am going to pursue this course, _____（无论我要作出什么样的牺牲）.

90. I would prefer shopping online to shopping in a department store because _____ _____（它更加方便和省时）.

91. Many Americans live on credit, and their quality of life _____（是用他们能够借到多少来衡量的）, not how much they can earn.

2007 年 12 月 22 日大学英语
四级考试 B 卷参考答案
COLLEGE ENGLISH TEST (Band Four)

Part I Writing

参考范文

Nowadays many college students prefer to have electives in their spare time because the courses can offer a variety of skills and abundant knowledge apart from what they learn in the daily courses. There are many factors that may account for it, and the following are the most conspicuous aspects.

To start with, many students want to get another degree besides their own, so that they can have more competence when they seek a job. Furthermore, as for me, I don't care about degree or job, I just want to obtain some necessary skills to make my college life worthwhile. What I'm concerned most is how to own more skills that may be necessary for my future. Finally, some students want to learn anything that is different from what they are learning now. The science students, for example, want to know about Shakespeare while the art students want to tell how a vehicle works and how to deal with it when it breaks down. So, they can all get what they think is useful to their college life.

On the whole, the phenomenon is one of the results of multi-demand of the employment market. There is still a long way for us to improve the elective itself, but as a student myself, I find it rewarding and interesting.

Part II Reading Comprehension (Skimming and Scanning)

1. C. a powerful force for global integration

2. B. at an annual rate of 3.9%

3. D. 20%.

4. A. They give them chances for international study or internship.

5. D. Yale's collaboration with Fudan University on genetic research

6. B. It was intentionally created by Standford University.

7. C. It has been unsteady for years.

8. changes in the visa process

9. take their knowledge and skills back home

10. strengthen the nation

Part III Listening Comprehension

Section A

11. D. She was somewhat overweight.

12. B. At the hotel reception.

13. A. Having confidence in her son.

14. A. Have a short break.

15. C. He has been in perfect condition.

16. D. She still keeps some old furniture in her new house.

17. A. The woman forget lending the book to the man.

18. B. The man doesn't look like a sportsman.

19. C. She has packed it in one of her bags.

20. B. It will last one week.

21. D. The taxi is waiting for them.

22. A. At home.

23. B. She is tired of her present work.

24. C. Translator.

25. D. Education and experience.

Section B

26. D. They care a lot about children.

27. C. Their birth information is usually kept secret.

28. B. They have mixed feelings about finding their natural parents.

29. A. Adoption has much to do with love.

30. B. He bought The Washington Post.

31. C. She was the first woman to lead a big U.S. publishing company.

32. A. Katharine had exerted an important influence on the world.

33. D. It'll protect them from possible financial crises.

34. D. They can't immediately get back the money paid for their medical cost.

35. C. They needn't pay the entire medical bill at once.

Section C

36. alarming   37. increased   38. sheer   39. disturbing   40. comparison

41. proportion   42. force   43. inverse

44. The percentage of people living in cities is much higher than the percentage working in industry.

45. There is not enough money to build adequate houses for the people that live there, let alone the new arrivals.

46. So the figures for the growth of towns and cities represent proportional growth of

148

unemployment and underemployment,

Part IV Reading Comprehension (Reading in Depth)

Section A

47. E. projects   48. C. role   49. O. acting   50. F. offers   51. L. cooperative

52. I. forward   53. J. especially   54. G. information   55. A. victims   56. K. entire

Section B

57. A. A lot of distractions compete for children's time nowadays.

58. D. Her way to success was full of pains and frustrations.

59. B. She wanted to share her stories with readers.

60. D. She believed she had the knowlede and experience to offer guidance.

61. C. Children should be allowed freedom to grow through experience.

62. B. All its courses are offered online.

63. C. a minimum or total absence of face-to-face instruction

64. A. save a great deal on traveling and boarding expenses

65. C. The evaluation system used by online universities is inherently weak.

66. D. cutting down on their expenses

Part V Cloze

67. C. as   68. B. to   69. D. distinguished   70. B. related   71. A. In

72. C. much   73. A. behavior   74. D. but   75. B. negative   76. C. given

77. D. consistent   78. B. consumers   79. C. favorable   80. A. Moreover   81. D. enhancing

82. B. readily   83. A. volume   84. C. amount   85. C. intentions   86. A. turn

Part VI Translation

87. Thanks to a series of new inventions

88. I am more likely to get tired than before

89. whatever sacrifice I have to make

90. it is more convenient and less time-consuming

91. is measured by how much they can loan

2007 年 12 月 22 日大学英语
四级考试 B 卷听力原文
COLLEGE ENGLISH TEST（Band Four）

Part III Listening Comprehension

Section A

11. M: I ran into Sally the other day. I could hardly recognize her. Do you remember her from

high school?

M: Yeah, she was a little out of shape back then. Well, has she lost a lot of weight?

Q: What does the man remember of Sally?

12. W: We don't seem to have a reservation for you, sir. I'm sorry.

M: But my secretary said that she had reserved a room for me here. I phoned her from the airport this morning just before I got on board the plane.

Q: Where does the conversation most probably take place?

13. W: What would you do if you were in my place?

M: If Paul were my son, I'd just not worry. Now that his teacher is giving him extra help and he's working hard himself, he's sure to do well in the next exam.

Q: What's the man's suggestion to the woman?

14. M: You've had your hands full and have been overworked during the last two weeks. I think you really need to go out and get some fresh air and sunshine.

W: You are right. That's just what I'm thinking about.

Q: What is the woman most probably going to do?

15. W: Hello, John. How are you feeling now? I hear you've been ill.

M: They must have confused me with my twin brother Rods. He's been sick all week, but I've never felt better in my life.

Q: What do we learn about the man?

16. M: Did you really give away all your furniture when you moved into the new house last month?

W: Just the useless pieces, as I'm planning to purchase a new set from Italy for the sitting room only.

Q: What does the woman mean?

17. M: I've brought back your *Oxford Companion to English Literature*. I thought you might use it for your paper. Sorry not to have returned it earlier.

W: I was wondering where that book was.

Q: What can we infer from the conversation?

18. W: To tell the truth, Tony, it never occurs to me that you are an athlete.

M: Oh, really? Most people who meet me, including some friends of mine, don't think so either.

Q: What do we learn from the conversation?

Conversation One

W: Mary, I hope you're packed and ready to leave.

W: Yes, I'm packed, but not quite ready. I can't find my passport.

M: Your passport? That's the one thing you mustn't leave behind.

150

W: I know. I haven't lost it. I've packed it, but I can't remember which bag it's in.

M: Well, you have to find it at the airport. Come on, the taxi is waiting.

W: Did you say taxi? I thought we were going in your car.

M: Yes, well, I have planned to, but I'll explain later. You've got to be there in an hour.

W: The plane doesn't leave for two hours. Anyway, I'm ready to go now.

M: Now, you're taking just one case, is that right?

W: No, there is one in the hall as well.

M: Gosh, what a lot of stuff! You're taking enough for a month instead of a week.

W: Well, you can't depend on the weather. It might be cold.

M: It's never cold in Rome. Certainly not in May. Come on, we really must go.

W: Right, we're ready. We've got the bags, I'm sure there's no need to rush.

M: There is. I asked the taxi driver to wait two minutes, not twenty.

W: Look, I'm supposed to be going away to relax. You're making me nervous.

M: Well, I want you to relax on holiday, but you can't relax yet.

W: OK, I promise not to relax, at least not until we get to the airport and I find my passport.

Questions 19 to 22 are based on the conversation you have just heard.

19. What does the woman say about her passport?

20. What do we know about the woman's trip?

21. Why does the man urge the woman to hurry?

22. Where does the conversation most probably take place?

Conversation Two

W: Oh, I'm fed up with my job.

M: Hey, there's a perfect job for you in the paper today. You might be interested.

W: Oh, what is it? What do they want?

M: Wait a minute. Uh, here it is. The European Space Agency is recruiting translators.

W: The European Space Agency?

M: Well, that's what it says. They need an English translator to work from French or German.

W: So they need a degree in French or German, I suppose. Well, I've got that. What's more, I have plenty of experience. What else are they asking for?

M: Just that. A university degree and three or four years of experience as a translator in a professional environment. They also say the person should have a lively and inquiring mind, effective communication skills and the ability to work individually or as a part of the team.

W: Well, if I stay at my present job much longer, I won't have any mind or skills left. By the way, what about salary? I just hope it isn't lower than what I get now.

M: It's said to be negotiable. It depends on the applicant's education and experience. In addition to basic salary, there's a list of extra benefits. Have a look yourself.

151

W: Hm, travel and social security plus relocation expenses are paid. Hey, this isn't bad. I really want the job.

Questions 23 to 25 are based on the conversation you have just heard.

23. Why is the woman trying to find a new job?

24. What position is being advertised in the paper?

25. What are the key factors that determine the salary of the new position?

Section B

Passage One

When couples get married, they usually plan to have children. Sometimes, however, a couple can not have a child of their own. In this case, they may decide to adopt a child. In fact, adoption is very common today. There are about 60 thousand adoptions each year in the United States alone. Some people prefer to adopt infants, others adopt older children, some couples adopt children from their own countries, others adopt children from foreign countries. In any case, they all adopt children for the same reason — they care about children and want to give their adopted child a happy life.

Most adopted children know that they are adopted. Psychologists and child-care experts generally think this is a good idea. However, many adopted children or adoptees have very little information about their biological parents. As a matter of fact, it is often very difficult for adoptees to find out about their birth parents because the birth records of most adoptees are usually sealed. The information is secret so no one can see it. Naturally, adopted children have different feelings about their birth parents. Many adoptees want to search for them, but others do not. The decision to search for birth parents is a difficult one to make. Most adoptees have mixed feelings about finding their biological parents. Even though adoptees do not know about their natural parents, they do know that their adopted parents want them, love them and will care for them.

Questions 26 to 29 are based on the passage you have just heard.

26. According to the speaker, why do some couples adopt children?

27. Why is it difficult for adoptees to find out about their birth parents?

28. Why do many adoptees find it hard to make the decision to search for their birth parents?

29. What can we infer from the passage?

Passage Two

Katherine Gram graduated from University of Chicago in 1938 and got a job as a news reporter in San Francisco. Katherine's father used to be a successful investment banker. In 1933, he bought a failing newspaper, the Washington Post.

Then Katherine returned to Washington and got a job, editing letters in her father's newspaper. She married Philip Gram, who took over his father-in-law's position shortly after and became publisher of the Washington Post. But for many years, her husband suffered from mental illness and he killed himself in 1963. After her husband's death, Katherine operated the newspaper. In the 1970s, the newspaper became famous around the world and Katherine was also recognized as an important leader in newspaper publishing. She was the first woman to head a major American publishing company, the Washington Post company. In a few years, she successfully expanded the company to include newspaper, magazine, broadcast and cable companies.

She died of head injuries after a fall when she was 84. More than 3 thousand people attended her funeral including many government and business leaders. Her friends said she would be remembered as a woman who had an important influence on events in the United States and the world. Katherine once wrote, "The world without newspapers would not be the same kind of world". After her death, the employees of the Washington Post wrote, "The world without Katherine would not be the same at all."

Questions 30 to 32 are based on the passage you have just heard.

30. What do we learn from the passage about Katherine's father?

31. What does the speaker tell us about Katherine Gram?

32. What does the comment by employees of the Washington Post suggest?

Passage Three

Obtaining good health insurance is a real necessity while you are studying overseas. It protects you from minor and major medical expenses that can wipe out not only your savings but your dreams of an education abroad. There are often two different types of health insurance you can consider buying, international travel insurance and student insurance in the country where you will be going.

An international travel insurance policy is usually purchased in your home country before you go abroad. It generally covers a wide variety of medical services and you are often given a list of doctors in the area where you will travel who may even speak your native language. The drawback might be that you may not get your money back immediately, in other words, you may have to pay all your medical expenses and then later submit your receipts to the insurance company.

On the other hand, getting student heath insurance in the country where you will study might allow you to only pay a certain percentage of the medical cost at the time of service and thus you don't have to have sufficient cash to pay the entire bill at once. Whatever you decide, obtaining some form of health insurance is something you should consider before you go overseas. You shouldn't wait until you are sick with major medical bills to pay off.

Questions 33 to 35 are based on the passage you have just heard.

33. Why does the speaker advice overseas students to buy health insurance?

34. What is the drawback of students buying international travel insurance?
35. What does the speaker say about students getting health insurance in the country where they will study?

Section C

More and more of the world's population are living in towns or cities. The speed at which cities are growing in the less developed countries is alarming. Between 1920 and 1960, big cities in developed countries increased two and a half times in size, but in other parts of the world the growth was eight times their size. The sheer size of growth is bad enough, but there are now also very disturbing signs of trouble in the comparison of percentages of people living in towns and percentages of people working in industry. During the 19th century, cities grew as a result of the growth of industry. In Europe, the proportion of people living in cities was always smaller than that of the work force working in factories. Now, however, the reverse is almost always true in the newly industrialized world. The percentage of people living in cities is much higher than the percentage working in industry. Without a base of people working in industry, these cities cannot pay for their growth. There is not enough money to build adequate houses for the people that live there, let alone the new arrivals. There has been little opportunity to build water supplies or other facilities. So the figures for the growth of towns and cities represent proportional growth of unemployment and underemployment, a growth in the number of hopeless and despairing parents and starving children.